Praise for *Zorrie*
Finalist for the 2021 National Book Award in Fiction

"A virtuosic portrait of midcentury America itself. . . . What Hunt ultimately gives us is a pure and shining book, an America where community becomes a 'symphony of souls,' a sustenance greater than romance or material wealth for those wise enough to join in."
—*The New York Times*

"Through an ordinary life of hard work and simple pleasures, Zorrie comes to learn the real wonder is life itself. A quiet, beautifully done, and memorable novel." —*Library Journal,* **starred review**

"Packs a whole, absorbing human life into just 161 pages that are polished like jewels." **—Scott Simon, NPR**

"A touching, tightly woven story from an always impressive author." —*Kirkus,* **"Best Books of 2021"**

"A powerful portrait of longing and community in the American Midwest. . . . Hunt chronicles the events of Zorrie's life with swiftness and precision, [and] a quiet sensitivity rarely seen in American fiction." —*BookPage*

"Hunt celebrates the majesty and depth in a life that may superficially seem undistinguished. . . . A beautifully written ode to the rural Midwest." —*Booklist*

"Through loss, grief, and tragedy, Hunt's lyrical and intimate novel shows that life is not a sum of its negative experiences but a collection of joyful moments." —*Shelf Awareness*

"This is not just a book you are holding in your hands; it is a life. Laird Hunt gives us here the portrait of a woman painted with the finest brush imaginable, while also rendering great historical shifts with bold single strokes. A poignant, unforgettable novel, *Zorrie* is Hunt at his best." **—Hernan Diaz**

"Hunt's novel reads like poetry, evoking writers like Paul Harding and Marilynne Robinson, and radiates the heat of a beating heart."
　　　　　　　　　　　　　　　　　　　　　　　　　　—*Vox*

Selected Praise for Laird Hunt

"There is always a surprise in the voice and in the heart of Laird Hunt's stories—with their echoes of habit caught in a timeless dialect, so we see the world he gives us as if new."
　　　　　　　　　　　　—Michael Ondaatje on *Kind One*

"A vivid, disturbing book. . . . Mature, accomplished, impressive."
　　　　　　　　　　　　—Hilary Mantel on *The Evening Road*

"A spare, beautiful novel, so deeply about America and the language of America that its sentences seem to rise up from the earth itself. Laird Hunt had me under his spell from the first word of *Neverhome* to the last. Magnificent."　　**—Paul Auster on** *Neverhome*

"A brilliant and breathtaking blaze of a novel. . . . A slim and unshowy story of devastating power, an epic poem in its own vernacular, an upside-down *Odyssey* at once particular and hauntingly universal."　　　　　　　　　　**—The Guardian on** *Neverhome*

"Hunt's novels shimmer and shift like reflections on wind-stirred water. . . . An edgy and labyrinthine tale of longing, madness, and death."　　　　　　　　　　　　　**—Booklist on** *The Exquisite*

"Hunt brings to mind Flannery O'Connor's grotesques and Barry Hannah's bracingly inventive prose and cranks. He is strange, challenging, and a joy to read."　　　　**—Kirkus on** *The Evening Road*

"As devastating a piece of writing as anything one is likely to find in contemporary literature."
　　　　　　　　—Review of Contemporary Fiction on *Kind One*

INDIANA, INDIANA

ALSO BY LAIRD HUNT

INDIANA, INDIANA

(the dark and lovely portions of the night)

Laird Hunt

COFFEE HOUSE PRESS
Minneapolis
2023

Coffee House Press books are available to the trade through our primary distributor, Consortium Book Sales & Distribution, cbsd.com or (800) 283-3572. For personal orders, catalogs, or other information, write to info@coffeehousepress.org.

Coffee House Press is a nonprofit literary publishing house. Support from private foundations, corporate giving programs, government programs, and generous individuals helps make the publication of our books possible. We gratefully acknowledge their support in detail in the back of this book.

LIBRARY OF CONGRESS CATALOGING-IN-PUBLICATION DATA

Names: Hunt, Laird, author.
Title: Indiana, indiana / Laird Hunt.
Description: Minneapolis : Coffee House Press, 2023.
Identifiers: LCCN 2022039181 (print) | LCCN 2022039182
    (ebook) | ISBN 9781566896658 (paperback) | ISBN
    9781566896665 (epub)
Classification: LCC PS3608.U58 I5 2023 (print) |
    LCC PS3608.U58 (ebook) | DDC 813/.6—dc23
LC record available at https://lccn.loc.gov/2022039181
LC ebook record available at https://lccn.loc.gov/2022039182

PRINTED IN THE UNITED STATES OF AMERICA

30 29 28 27 26 25 24 23   1 2 3 4 5 6 7 8

For Helen Burnau Hunt
Grandma
(1912–2002)
Much loved, much missed

What strange and unlikely things are
washed up on the shore of time.
—*William Maxwell*
So Long, See You Tomorrow

trails of fire, dews of blood . . .
—Hamlet *1.1*

INTRODUCTION

By Azareen Van der Vliet Oloomi

Born in Singapore in 1968, Laird Hunt lived in London, The Hague, and San Francisco before moving to his grandmother's farm in Clinton County, Indiana, where he attended Clinton Central High School. The farm has been in the Hunt family since before the Civil War, when the county population hovered around fourteen thousand, rising to thirty thousand in sluggish increments over the course of the twentieth century. Green and lush in summers, Clinton County has harsh winters that tend to stubbornly linger into the spring. It is a far cry from the urban epicenters the teenage Laird Hunt would have been used to in the great cosmopolitan metropolises of Europe. In rural Indiana, the passage of time—the feel of a day's arc and duration—diametrically opposes the dynamism and speed of urban life. The landscape demands a singular attention patiently trained on the natural world, resists restlessness, perhaps even mocks it. In turn, it offers sweet corn, mulberry trees, lowing cows, an explosion of flowers in the verdant summers, red cardinals that momentarily break the winter monolith, their bright rouge plumes a stark contrast to the glistening sheet of snow that drapes over the county—an icy, forbidding soporific.

The National Book Award finalist *Zorrie* (Hunt's latest) and the much earlier elegiac novel *Indiana, Indiana* (Hunt's first novel written and the second to be published) are both set in Clinton County, Indiana—the site of Hunt's own displaced adolescence, where he suddenly found himself in the aftermath of a shift in the fault lines of his family, cordoned off from the agile luxury of South Kensington in London. The sudden silence must have been deafening.

One could say that *Indiana, Indiana* is *Zorrie*'s literary ancestor. Like Russian nested dolls, the two novels share a constellation of characters. The protagonist of *Indiana, Indiana,* Noah Summers, is paid a series of visits by his neighbor, Zorrie, late in the novel. By then, Noah has burnt down the family barn in a last-ditch effort to be rejoined with the great love of his life, Opal, who was locked away in Logansport State Hospital due to her penchant for setting things on fire. Forbidden by her guardians from receiving Noah, the man to whom she was briefly, albeit informally married, as a visitor, she writes letters to him all her life long, letters full of passion and pathos. Opal, with her idiosyncratic speech, charcoal hair, and blueberry eyes, appears in *Zorrie,* as does Noah Summers. What is true of Zorrie is true of Noah Summers too: "It was Indiana, it was the dirt she had bloomed up out of, it was who she was, what she felt, how she thought, what she knew."

Where *Zorrie* is told in limpid, efficient prose that progresses at a refined gallop and exists on a continuum with the fine domestic realism of Flaubert's *A Simple Heart, Indiana, Indiana* is told in a polyphonic delirium, an incantatory whirlwind that disorients us as it strives to deliver Noah from the pain of his separation from Opal, the stinging knowledge that his beloved is being treated to ice baths and electroshock therapy in the cold confines of the state hospital from which he is barred. It is a tender, youthful novel, an ode to devotional romantic love that seems almost otherworldly in its innocence and to the quiet gothic landscape of Indiana, as benevolent as it is unsettling.

Indiana, Indiana is infused with a stilled and halted sense of time and a weighted silence. There's a haunted quality to the prose. The characters speak to one another in ghostly whispers across the vast physical and spiritual distances that separate them. Noah's father, Virgil, is prone to disappearances and, not unlike his son, tends to sink into periods of sustained withdrawal. "Talk. Not talk. Virgil alternated between the two until, the last few years of his life, he stopped talking entirely, as if, it seemed to Noah, he had slipped into a layer that was much deeper than most. Now Noah, who has never been much of a talker, has also mostly stopped. Sometimes, he talks to Max. Sometimes, he talks to himself—holds long, unpleasant conversations aloud in the dark." The further Noah retreats, the louder the voices he overhears become. "At times, the voices are very loud and sharp, and hearing them makes Noah feel wide awake and a little sick." These voices, too, are shot through with silence. "The voice that talks is deep and slow and often in the middle of this voice there are silences that fall through Noah's head like warm round stones."

In this respect, *Indiana, Indiana* shares a spectral quality with Juan Rulfo's classic novel, *Pedro Páramo*, in which the main character, Juan Preciado, travels to his deceased mother's birthplace in search of his father only to find himself wandering through a ghost town. Both novels are allegorical; the reader is drawn into a long vigil, a place of mourning that, in *Indiana, Indiana,* is utterly particular to Noah Summers but also universal: a story of love and loss and of the deep strangeness of living in rural America. What is perhaps most fascinating about Hunt's novels—and *Indiana, Indiana* is no exception—is the way that he brings the aesthetic traditions of continental modernity to bear on rural America, recovering and recentering its marginalized geographies in our collective imaginary.

The two Indiana novels, the earlier fragmented and kaleidoscopic novel and the later stately novel of elegant realism, form a Möbius strip that readers can move across pleasurably as they come to know the characters in their dual manifestations. In *Zorrie*, Noah Summers is a reliable friend and neighbor, Zorrie's capable and trustworthy farmhand. In *Indiana, Indiana,* we see a pained Noah as he sits in vigil before the fire, hands to his face, recalling throughout the course of one night a lifetime of memories. Opal is the axis on which his visions turn. Her letters arrive like gusts of wind and are folded into the larger fabric of the text. Her voice is never muted. It is as limpid and clearly sung as Zorrie's is when she gets to occupy center stage in her own novel.

In Opal's letters the world is always askew; the elements blend into each other, the boundaries between people and places and things are blurred to irrelevance. She writes to Noah: "Then I grew and you stretched. I told the doctor. I said our heads dripped into each other." This image is echoed marvelously in the final stretch of the novel, when we see Noah and Opal visit a cave where stalactites and stalagmites "grow together in beautiful pink columns." The two are on their honeymoon, and for a moment we get to see them together as they glide through the underground waters on a boat, perfectly content to keep company with each other. The disorientation of the first half of the novel begins to crystalize as we learn in clear precise prose what was lost. We register Noah's shock as he comes home to see a calm Opal sitting at the kitchen table after she has set the curtains on fire. As the house burns down, she asks him what he wants for supper.

The Noah we see in *Indiana, Indiana* is partially literate and, like the biblical Noah, pure of heart, innocent; he is also mildly clairvoyant, prone after Opal's departure to Logansport to precognitive experiences. At one point he sees a clock standing taller than himself and Virgil, its pendulum swinging auspiciously, at the edge of the field. He sees log cabins that had been knocked down three quarters of a century before. He sees "an old man in deer skins holding an antler in one hand." His character brings to mind a famous line by the Catalan writer J. V. Foix, "When I sleep then I see clearly." At first, he dreams things while he is awake, but as time moves forward and backward in elliptical leaps and folds, he begins to have visions in his sleep.

This opacity of character exists also in his father. Like Dante's guide through the inferno, Noah's father, Virgil, speaks in literary riddles. "Fifty percent meaning, Virgil more than once explained, that at best only about fifty percent of the story came clear. . . . But that fifty percent, even if it took you half your whole life to get at it, Virgil had continued, *was* there." Sense and senselessness, sanity and pathos, linear and elliptical time, sound and silence, coexist in *Indiana, Indiana,* not in antagonistic blocks or as oppositional binaries but as part of an aesthetic and psychological spectrum that preserves the dignity and sovereignty of the characters, all of whom are prone to eccentricities that seem to bloom out of the rural landscape with the same fierce authenticity that Zorrie, in all her resilience and integrity, bloomed up out of Indiana.

In both novels the nature of memory and the passage of time exist in perfect symbiosis. And both novels are infused not only with silence, but with a sense of loneliness and isolation. Noah Summers does not float up on the floodwaters with a wife and a community of animals. He is, in many ways, utterly alone. "There was another Noah, one who had also built a fine enough ship at God's bidding, only to his ark no animals came. Nor did wife or child come and when he searched the hills and dales he found that all those he had known and loved in his life had vanished."

This elliptical and allegorical temporality is anchored by references to global history and to concrete images of the passage of time. In *Zorrie* we see the ghost girls, licking the tips of their paint brushes as they paint glow-in-the-dark numbers on clockfaces at the Radium Dial Company. Harold, Zorrie's husband, enlists as an Army Air Corps navigator and is shot down by German artillery in December 1943. He dies on the coast of Holland. In *Indiana, Indiana,* Noah Summers delivers mail during WWII, when postmen were in short supply. Clocks are ever present; they appear often throughout the narrative, a motif device that seems to insist that this landscape is of our time and worthy of our attention. In one of his visions, Noah sees Opal and the angels wearing photographs of clocks. "I lost time," he says, "and could not find it again." But "there are moments when he can hear it, quite clearly ticking, as if the fields were preparing to explode."

In Hunt's able hands, forsaken American landscapes are made legible in all their insularity and elusiveness. In all of Hunt's novels, place acts as an anchor. He has an uncanny capacity for capturing rural America on the page and for conveying to his readers a subtle understanding of how integral to our history, our national ideals, and our place in the global order the supposedly minor lives of its inhabitants are. He writes with an earnest, steady hand and with a gravity and nuance reminiscent of Cormac McCarthy and John Steinbeck. Language is his vehicle for returning to the dirt that he, like Noah and Zorrie, knows and thinks about. He tills the soil with words over and over again, until it reveals itself to us through characters who are so proximate to the earth that they are indivisible from it. "It's all so beautiful," Opal writes. "Indiana is beautiful. Indiana where the lilacs are flowering, Indiana where the furrows are sprouting fire-flies and corn." Hunt's Indiana novels are books of great beauty, even ecstasy. Lucky us that the Indiana landscape may just be his private elixir.

INDIANA, INDIANA

NOAH HOLDS HIS HANDS UP TO THE FIRE. Later, when it is light, and the Sun has begun to burn the blue edges off the new snow, Noah will take the saw, leave the shed, and set out across the field. But now it is still dark outside. And it is cold. Noah holds his hands in front of the fire until they are hot, then pulls them away and covers his face. Through the gaps where his fingers are gone Noah can see the stove, and, on the low table beside it, the chipped blue bowl filled with water. Noah takes his hands away from his face, reaches into the breast pocket of his coveralls, retrieves a paper flower, inspects it, then drops it into the bowl. Nothing. The green and orange flower swells a little, then, without opening, not even a little, begins to sink. Noah is surprised. Just yesterday Max dropped two of the flowers into the bowl, and together they watched them unfold and darken and expand across the surface of the water into brilliant blooms. Noah fishes the packet of "Japanese Precious Beauty Flowers" out of his pocket and inspects it. One corner of the packet, which Max pulled out from under a pile of broken light bulbs and used peat pots at the far end of the room, has been nibbled open and a few of the flowers have been chewed, but Noah can't see anything wrong with the rest of them. Defective, Noah thinks. Or too old. He wonders if at some point in the years since he received the gold and silver packet a little oil, or some other substance, might have seeped in, spoiling most of the flowers, but they are so small that it is difficult to tell. Noah shrugs and starts to set the packet aside, then changes his mind, leans forward, dumps the remaining flowers into the bowl, puts his hands back over his face, and watches. Same result. Only now upward of a dozen of the waterlogged multi-colored flowers float at different levels beneath the surface, and after a time it occurs to Noah that although this result is not what he had hoped for, it is by no means unpleasant. Noah stretches his arms out and yawns. He is still a little chilled, so that what begins as a yawn ends as a deep shiver, but the room is growing warmer and his face is no longer so cold. He leans forward, lifts a chunk of wood off the pile, and throws it into the stove. Sparks fly. Noah's eyes move between the bits of submerged paper in the blue bowl and the new piece of wood as the fire rises around it. The cold wood takes the heat slowly, almost patiently. A ridge of orange flame forms along the top, and the colors in the bowl shift. They continue to shift. Light then dark then back to light again.

Dear Noah,

Last week I had a pretty dream in which you came to my room with a bag of bright red apples. Then my room was a bright green valley sloping downward and at the bottom was an apple tree filled with apples like the one they have here in the yard. Today the sky was blue and I saw my eye while they were doing something to me, it was orange with six red lines. A boy comes in the evenings and reads to us. In the book they are having a dance on a field above the ocean. Everybody's up over the ocean. Everybody's wearing masks. They dance and wave their arms and look at each other, then they take off their masks, and it's pretty because with the masks off it's all new and they don't know who anyone is. I wonder why my eye was orange. I am sending you some flowers. They're like real flowers because they need water. What are you doing? I keep hoping, dear Noah, that I'll have that same dream.

Love, Opal

NOAH IS TIRED. He never sleeps well in the winter, and tonight Max came over late carrying a cardboard box under his arm. Max walked right into the bedroom, right over to the bed where Noah had been lying wide awake with his eyes shut, and put the box in Noah's hands. He smiled at Noah, stood there smiling for a moment, said, it's in there, I didn't want to get snow on it, then turned without saying anything else, and walked out. A few minutes later, Noah got out of bed, pulled on his coveralls, took a piece of dark cloth out of Ruby's old bureau, carried the box out to the shed, and got a fire going in the stove. For a time he just sat there trying to get warm after crossing the cold, snow-filled barn lot, then he remembered the bowl and the packet of flowers and thought it would be nice, since there was still a lot of night left and no need to be in a hurry about anything, to watch a few more of them open and spread across the water's surface.

Now the packet is empty, and the bowl has been set off to the side, and Noah sits contemplating the box. It is beside him on top of a pile of nails, bolts, and used spark plugs that Noah has covered with the piece of dark cloth. There is a similar cloth covering the family Bible that sits on a table in the library. The Bible is an 1867 large-print illustrated text in parallel column King James in which, in a variety of hands, are recorded the birth and death dates of many of the members of Noah's family, with just enough space left at the bottom of the page for a couple more.

Reverend James Franklin 1830–1870
Captain Frank Keller 1851–1885
Eloise Franklin Keller 1856–1885
Mabel Thatcher Franklin 1838–1903
Johnson Richard Summers 1879–1906

Robert Summers 1854–1909
Minnie James Summers 1859–1921
Sylvie Agnes Keller Jackson 1884–1958
Virgil Bayard Summers 1877–1966
Ruby Louise Keller Summers 1880–1970

Pressed oak, birch, hickory, and maple leaves are scattered throughout the Old Testament, and pressed pansies, each with its own tiny envelope of waxed paper, throughout the New. The bible is bound in black, gold-embossed, ridged leather, and it weighs sixteen and a half pounds. Seventy-seven years ago Noah spent three hours in the chicken house for leaving it sitting on the scales, and he can still hear the soft clucking and scratching of the chickens, the whirring and settling of wings. Now the chicken house is empty of all but a few dozen cobalt mason jars. Seven of them sit in a row on the windowsill and, in the morning, when the Sun is shining, throw a slowly descending bar of blue light onto the corrugated walls, the recent sight of which, although he is not sure why, made Noah shiver. Noah shivers. The voices have come. Virgil is speaking. He pulls his hand away from the box and leans back in his chair. Listen. This is a good one. The first moving picture I ever saw was in a tent a couple of fellows out of Indianapolis had set up on the South End of the old fairgrounds in Kirklin. The picture wasn't much bigger than the one we watch the news on now and the tent was so small they could only let five or six in at a time. You put a nickel in the jar and then they'd let you in. The projection lasted about two minutes and was accomplished by means of a crank they'd take turns at. One hand on the crank, one hand on their cigar. They were about the greasiest pair of cusses we'd ever seen and if we had known any better we would have figured out that they didn't know more than the second thing about operating one of those machines but we didn't know any better and we just paid the nickel and went in. And there it was. It didn't matter if it did keep speeding up and slowing down and even stopping dead still when they changed turns. There it was. I can't even remember exactly what it was except that there was a man having trouble with a garden hose. It didn't matter what it was. I put five nickels in their jar and would have put five more in if the authorities hadn't come and arrested them for possession of stolen property. They'd done ten towns in ten nights. I thought about that afterwards. About a machine like that being stolen. About them showing that picture and taking nickels and more nickels and the authorities after them and everyone seeing moving pictures for the first time. I thought about it and it started seeming like it was the nickels themselves that were being shot out of the machine and stamped out fresh one after another in that light. Afterwards I say. I did all my thinking about it afterwards. You paid the plain old nickel and you went in the tent. There were seats and you sat down and everyone was talking and then everyone got quiet and leaned forward. After the first couple of rounds all you could hear in the tent was that crank handle and your own breathing. It was like the world was happening all over again on a square of white canvas in front of your eyes.

VIRGIL—FATHER, PAPA, PÈRE. Before he married and became a farmer, Virgil was a schoolteacher and regular fixture at parties and social clubs and wherever there was any discussion taking place—anywhere. Once, he liked to note, preferably while brandishing a torn and yellowed program that eventually, for the sake of its preservation, had to be retired, he had been paid fifteen dollars to deliver a self-titled address on the "Indisputable Advantages of According Adequate Attention to the Classics, with Due Emphasis on the Latins and Excellent Commentary on the Greeks" to a Gay Club gathering attended by the County Commissioner, the Mayor of Frankfort, and the Principal of Kirklin High School. Virgil was also fond of mentioning that he had spent three semesters studying at Indiana University, where he had, after the fashion of the old orators, developed his passion for talk.

We are all of us, he once said, composed of layers, like rock strata or a variety of discrete liquids in a closed system or the primary colors in a spectrum (there now, see them? aren't they pretty? [a six-inch rainbow was suddenly sitting before Noah on the kitchen table]) or the varied textures of dirt in an Indian burial mound. I find talking a necessary, even complementary adjunct to the considerably longer periods of silence in which you will find we are all of us forced to indulge.

Talk. Not talk. Virgil alternated between the two until, the last few years of his life, he stopped talking entirely, as if, it seemed to Noah, he had slipped into a layer that was deeper than most. Now Noah, who has never been much of a talker, has also mostly stopped. Sometimes, he talks to Max. Sometimes, he talks to himself—holds long, unpleasant conversations aloud in the dark. Noah prefers talking to Max. Or to the cats.

Cats, for example, he says. Cats, come here. Sit with me. Sit close.

Mostly, though, Noah listens. To Max, to the cats, to the radio, to the voices that with greater and greater frequency come to occupy his head. At times, the voices are very loud and sharp, and hearing them makes Noah feel wide awake and a little sick. Other times they are soft with big curved edges like the French horns his mother Ruby used to like to hear played on the Victrola when they would go to Aunt Sylvie's, years ago, years and years ago, and when Noah hears them he drifts.

Noah drifts.

Away from the junk-cluttered room on the north end of the shed on the north side of the farm in the center of the county in the center of Indiana in the heart of the country, and down a long dark hallway toward a brightly colored door. Often, lately, when he is entering sleep, faintly accelerating worlds like this one flow past him. Often, lately, as this occurs, and takes its course, he has had the sensation of being mounted, mounted on something very old, something that is preparing, whether he likes it or not, to gallop.

YOUR FATHER GOT IN AN AIRPLANE ONCE. I never did. I never did want to. It was some young fellow running an operation at the county fair. He had a bright red plane with a blue something on the side and the pilot was up out of Evansville and he had "Heaven or Bust" painted in yellow on both wings. I told your father I didn't like that and your father said, Well I intend to find out if he means it, and I asked your father what he meant by that and he kissed me and said, Hush, Ruby, and handed over his dollar. That boy in the goggles said, Ma'am I will bring you back a changed man, and I said never mind, but I guess maybe that's what he did. You should have heard your father after that—for weeks afterwards he would tell anyone he could corral that he had been on up to Heaven and it was pretty and empty and he had seen all he needed to see.

WAS IT COLD?
No.
Was it warm?
No, not warm either. Well, what was it like? Like I was a bird.
What kind of a bird?
A hawk. An eagle. A swallow. A dove. A buzzard. A bluebird. A robin. A wren.

Dear Noah,

Today I told the doctor that everything in my head was in bloom. The dogwood and the red bud were in bloom. The crab apple trees, cherry tree, and plum trees were in bloom. The bleeding heart was in bloom. The white and blue and yellow violets were in bloom. The spice bush was in bloom. The blue patch of hortensia by the hickory stump at the end of the clothesline was in bloom. The tulip bulbs we planted in the bed by the house were in bloom. The whole bed by the house was in bloom. The whole house before the fire and we were in it and we were in bloom.

Love, Opal

NOAH DRIFTS, THEN STOPS DRIFTING. His eyes come open. He blinks. A cat is sitting on the box, watching him. It watches while Noah leans forward, picks up another piece of wood, throws it into the open stove, then leans back again.

Cat, says Noah. You scrabbly old thing.

Max calls this one the Egyptian cat. Max has traveled. For a long time, Max said one evening as they were taking a turn around the yard, it seemed like the only comfortable thing to do. It just didn't sit right to let a place get too familiar.

Sit right how? Noah asked him.

I don't know, Max said. There wasn't all that much thought to it. I just kept moving. Whether it was the other side of the world or around the state. You ever do much traveling?

Never had much call to. I went down to Kentucky with the folks once. Then one other time. I took a long walk on one occasion. I don't know if that'd count.

Where'd you walk?

Up to Logansport.

When was this?

Before you were born.

That's a pretty good distance.

Yes it was.

Noah thought about it. He saw a campfire, a bat flicking through the dark, a diner with a heavy, pretty waitress, a puddle of sunlight, the poor, gray houses on the outskirts of town.

What was it like?

Noah didn't answer. Max did not repeat the question. Instead he asked, Is there anywhere you want to go now?

Noah looked at him.

How do you reckon?

I mean is there anywhere you would go if you could?

You saying you want to take me somewhere? On an outing or such?

Well, I don't know. I'm not sure. I've never exactly been on an outing, or at least never had what I was engaged in called that.

Noah chuckled. Max smiled. Then Noah said, There is one place.

Where's that?

Noah stood, left the room, was gone for quite some time, then returned with an envelope and handed it to Max.

You want me to look in this? Didn't I just hand it to you?

Max fished out the contents—a letter and a postcard that showed a hedge maze, a huge barn, a bend of blue river, and some kind of a structure that had no roof.

Read what she wrote, said Noah.

Max read:

Dear Noah,

We did finally take the trip to New Harmony that they had promised us. It is a lovely place. There is a church with no ceiling and grass for a floor and while they were singing I looked up at the clouds carrying on across the sky. We had such a pleasant time and we saw the rock where the angel stood and we ate very nice corn dogs by the Wabash. There was also a maze, which was so much fun except I couldn't get out right away and fell down. Well, we are back here now. The fellow who couldn't stop washing cars just died. I suppose he was old enough but I was sorry to hear about it. He used to whistle as he soaped up the cars.

Love, Opal

You want to go to New Harmony? said Max. Noah shrugged. Max stood.

I'll fetch you around 6:00 a.m.

They had a fine day. It was hot, but Max's car had air-conditioning and they made good time along the largely empty roads. They reached Terre Haute a little after 8:00, and stopped in Vincennes for coffee and an early lunch. Noah had brought along one of Virgil's old books: *Angel in the Forest,* by Marguerite Young, and as they worked over their turkey-melt specials, Max read aloud from it, about the Rappites then the Owenites and their successive contributions, along the banks of the Wabash, to the nineteenth-century American interest in reifying Utopian visions.

She's got some poet to her, this Marguerite Young, said Max.

That's what Virgil always said.

Did Virgil and Ruby get down there?

Church trip. They saw it before it got fixed back up. Ruby was disappointed some.

Max and Noah were not. The Sun beat down out of a blue sky and lit the restored structures and neat hedges and leaning grave markers with a fine clear light. There was a green pond with swans and mallards and a fine restaurant where they took their supper. They walked down to the Wabash and thought they saw a sandpiper, like Marguerite Young had described, and as they stood in the shade of an enormous sycamore, a raft with a crowd of girls and boys on it floated by. Later, they spent quite a while in the roofless church looking out the glassless windows or staring up at the sky. The rock where the angel had stood, setting the original holy community in motion, didn't seem like all that much to either of them, but both enjoyed the small maze and agreed that there was some trick to it.

I can see where she got pickled up, Noah said. I wonder where it was she fell down?

They took a stroll through the town, inspected a ceramics display, had a cup of coffee and a piece of pie.

You ready? said Max.

Noah nodded, although he wasn't quite ready. His mind was still working the little hedge maze, which Max had explained was mainly symbolic of humankind's earthly and spiritual struggle, and not necessarily meant to actually snag anyone up, although as they had both seen, it could. Noah couldn't stop thinking, as they headed to the car, about that snag and about getting pickled up and about minds that were nothing but great big pickle jars, his own not least of all, not by any means.

I'm glad we did that, it's a pretty place. I can see why she liked it, said Noah, his mind working the little maze, over and over as they drove away into a dusk that was rapidly turning the rolling countryside into a warm confabulation of border-less blues, browns, and grays, a merger that Noah, now sitting in the cold, stove-lit shed, finds it appealing to think of.

Just as he finds it appealing, leaning back in his chair and stretching his legs, to think of Max in motion, moving along the muddy banks of the Wabash, or from country to country, his long legs carrying him up strange mountains, through strange cities. Noah has seen some of the pictures Max took or had taken on his travels. A dark river lit by lanterns. Two small boys with brown teeth grinning in front of a large cat roasting on a spit. Max by a long, golden bridge. Max by a pyramid in the blazing Sun. Max by an old house with sagging gables. Max by a northern Indiana hospital bed. Max says there are cats a lot like this one that has now come to stand on Noah's lap and stare at him in the city of Cairo, and that there were cats like it in Egypt of old. He says that in special cases they built small pyramids to bury such cats, but that such pyramids are all long since drifted over with sand.

Virgil also knew about Egypt. Or said he did. He told Noah stories about Egyptian kings. All of the ones who weren't fed to crocodiles so that the crocodiles would emit gold and fertilize the great river were buried in tombs, Virgil said, some of which, like the small pyramids, were lost in sand or hidden in mountains, some of which were occasionally found.

For every piece of their lives that is still visible, said Virgil, there are thousands of pieces that are not. And that is not just a by-product of not finding something physically. You could hold what you think is an old chewed-up pig bone in your hands for your entire existence and have no idea or only a partial idea or most likely an absolutely aberrant idea of, say, just what wretched inference of your own ancestry you've found.

But what if it is just a pig bone?

Then it is just a pig bone. But think about it. It's still plenty strange.

Noah thought about it. And, engaged in the process of so thinking, for a time afterwards collected bones: sparrow, mouse, squirrel, gopher, chipmunk, lamb, robin, dog, possum, raccoon, crow, pigeon, deer, cardinal, cat, fish, rabbit, pig, lion, lemur, otter, rhino, gazelle, hyena, elephant, griffin, unicorn, hydra, hippogriff, phoenix (an unidentified rib bone he painted red).

Noah collected bones until Ruby found the box (labeled, with Virgil's help, "Strange Bones") in which he kept them, and he learned (she had found him with both hands in the box) that once bones no longer belonged to a body they were no longer clean.

Do you want to see one?

No I certainly do not.

You sure?

I'm sure.

Bones aren't clean?

What I said was bones are filthy.

What about when they're inside us?

Noah pulled his hands from behind his back and opened them, revealing a sparrow's skull and partially crushed wing. Virgil had just that morning called the one an empire and the other its own baffled retreat.

Ruby didn't answer, just stood there with her hands on her hips, frowning dubiously at the delicate white structures Noah was holding. After she was done frowning, and once or twice shaking her head, the bones, box and all, were sent out with Noah to the burning pile.

Noah, without telling Ruby, had other collections. Those included scraps of paper with green marks on them, dead insects, pieces of old clocks, color illustrations from books and magazines, and various accounts, clipped from newspapers or old novels, of what Virgil liked to call Fifty Percent Stories, which were mysterious things:

After a particularly fierce battle waged at the foot of the wall, the Emperor ordered rings drawn around all the corpses, Roman and Caledonian combined. His officers, in accordance with his will, filled 100 goatskin bags, fifty with black ash, fifty with iron oxide. After each ring was made, the corresponding corpse was removed. When the Emperor made his inspection the next day, more than three-quarters of the rings he found were overlapping. And if one paid close attention, the Emperor wrote near his death, it became clear that each imperfect ring, no matter how far removed from the others, was by some aspect of those others implied.

Fifty percent meaning, Virgil more than once explained, that at best only about fifty percent of the story came clear. And part of the time, the listener or reader didn't get even that fifty percent right away. But that fifty percent, even if it took you half your whole life to get at it, Virgil had continued, was there. Through observation and experiment, Noah has, in the case of some of Virgil's Fifty Percent Stories, found this to be accurate. When one autumn afternoon, for example, Virgil fell over in the kitchen, Noah, despite Ruby's protestations, sprinkled lime powder around him, and made sure the long, narrow ring stayed there until it had faded away. And when, in turn, one sunny winter morning Ruby died, Noah sprinkled an oval of corn around her bed. Separated by several years, five rooms, two hallways, and one flight of stairs, Noah found nothing immediately implicit at all in their relative positions at death. Two months ago, by the bedside at the rest home outside Logansport, however, after having widened the scope of the experiment by making a rectangle of long-stemmed roses around the edges of Opal's bed, it became clear to Noah that Virgil and Ruby had died almost side by side, almost in each other's arms.

Dear Noah,

Do you remember when we went to the cave? Do you remember how we walked down into the ground and the ceiling dripped and part of the time the drip was still and quiet and part of the time it was stone? I like how a drip can come up out of the floor. I know it doesn't really. But I like how it can. Do you know what I pretended? I told the doctor I was pretending. I pretended we were in the cave. I pretended I was on the ceiling and you were on the floor. I smiled and the smile dripped onto your head and stretched me and you grew. Then I grew and you stretched. I told the doctor. I said our heads had dripped into each other. He wrote this down on a pad. He said there was nothing wrong with this and had the nurse give me a glass of milk. He asked me if such thoughts made me happy or sad. I laughed. I told him I wanted to stand up and dance. I told him we were a single column now.

Love, Opal

NOAH HAS OPENED THE BOX. He has taken the mask out, pushed the box off to the side and set the mask in its place on the dark cloth. He has picked up the mask, set it down, and he has fussed around it and poked it with his finger. For a time, he stares at the mask and then, even though its features are obscured by all the paraphernalia he and Max had attached to it, he can't stand to stare any longer and turns away—it still feels too much like staring long and hard at his own face, a face he is eager, as he puts it to himself, to be shut of. Old faces for new, Noah thinks, then says aloud, the words shaping themselves into a warm spring evening more than sixty years ago.

He had finished up in the fields and was sitting on the front porch barefoot, cleaning off his boots, waiting for the good frying smells to come out of the kitchen and haul him in, when the old woman appeared and dropped her rucksack in front of him.

Got your supper coming I reckon, the old woman said.

She was tiny, with tight gray curls and crooked fingers, and looked too old to be walking around the countryside with a sack.

What can I do for you? said Noah.

You can acquaint yourself with my product line, said the old woman. And you can do yourself and the missus in there in the kitchen the favor of acquiring yourself some of it.

This was not the first time someone had come to the door of the little house on the west side of Virgil and Ruby's property with this and that to sell. More than one item had found its overpriced way into the house, and Virgil had felt himself obliged to address the issue.

I don't have any money, said Noah.

You sure about that? the old woman said. She had opened her rucksack and was holding a bottle in either hand. The bottles were made of purple glass and had brightly colored labels on them. The old woman shook the bottles and danced them around a moment in front of Noah's eyes.

What is it?

Ah, what is it not? said the woman and swam the bottles back and forth, over and above each other.

I don't have any money to spend, said Noah.

Well now no disrespect, none at all, but if you can't decide about spending your own money maybe I ought to talk to her in there that does.

She's getting supper.

I can smell it, said the old woman licking her lips. How much you asking?

A mere nickel each.

There anything in there besides water?

The old woman set one of the bottles down and unscrewed the lid on the other. She held it out to Noah and said, Smell.

That's pretty, said Noah.

It's a concoction. You can drink it or rub it on your arms. There's some wash the floor with it and others use it to scent up the privy. The missus will appreciate it. There's other feminine uses I could tell her about.

The old woman winked.

She's getting supper, Noah said. Fried chicken smells like.

Noah fished out a nickel. I'll take the one, he said.

Six cents for the two.

Noah shook his head.

I got other things, said the old woman, gesturing toward the sack. And not just things, but services too.

I got to get on in. I thank you. An old face for a new?

Noah had stood and started to turn away. He stopped.

A what? he said.

The old woman reached into her sack and brought out a bag of plaster.

I can make you a mold. A mold and then a mask. Of you or your missus or both. That ways you'll have your handsome young faces held and fixed forever.

How much?

Fifty cents. Seventy-five'll get you both put in plaster.

Noah laughed.

The old woman shrugged.

What's that about old faces for new? I don't follow.

That's just something I say to get their attention.

Doesn't have any particular sense to it?

The old woman shrugged. It might.

Well, I thank you anyway, said Noah.

Well, said the old woman.

Noah turned and started to walk into the house with the purple bottle and, as he did so, an image flashed into his mind of two masks, cunningly made, one for each of them, only the faces he saw represented in the masks, their faces, were old, terribly old. Noah staggered a little, fell against the doorway, then righted himself and turned back toward the old woman.

But the old woman had gone.

When, during a period in his life, Noah felt particularly troubled, he took up the habit of counting softly aloud from one to ten, over and over, until a clear stream of numbers filled his head.

One to ten is a pretty stretch, Virgil had once told him. It's a nice distance, as long or as short as you like. Say one and then breathe. Say two and then breathe. Get to know it.

Noah knows it.

He looks at the mask. He counts.

He breathes.

The room around his voice and breath becomes very quiet.

Noah, looking at the mask, counts into the cold, softly crackling room and when he stops counting the Egyptian cat sits dozing in his lap. Noah runs his hand through its thick fur. It purrs. It purrs deeply and slowly, and after a time it seems to Noah, as it has often seemed, that he has a soft, warm machine sitting on his lap.

Well, scrabbly cat? says Noah. You got anything interesting and out of the ordinary to say for yourself ? Anything in particular you would like at this moment to communicate?

The cat shifts, stretches, yawns, and settles.

Noah tries to remember the last time he gave it a dead rabbit or squirrel or bird, and can't.

I'm sorry, he says.

The cat says nothing.

I'll ask Max to get you one, he says. Or I'll get you one.

The cat looks up at him, yawns again, then slowly shuts its eyes.

Well, anyway, Max'll get you one. Don't worry. He'll do it if I ask him to. You just wait. The cat requires her some meat, I'll tell him. I'll set out a note.

ONCE UPON A TIME, NOAH HAD A JOB.

It was a pleasant job, and it made Noah happy, but, as Virgil put it afterward, Noah was not at his best during that period, and it did not last long.

No, we are sorry, said the Postmaster's assistant to Noah who, for a brief period of time during the war, was a postal carrier. We have had several complaints and we can't have several complaints. You can't monkey around with the United States Mail. We have already explained it to your father.

Virgil had arranged the job. He knew Hank Dunn in Frankfort and Hank Dunn knew the Postmaster and the Postmaster, who was short several carriers because of events in Europe and the Pacific, took care of it.

They had a fellow ride along with Noah the first few days and that fellow explained that it didn't particularly matter that Noah couldn't read or could only read very slowly, because all the mail had been separated and put in order, and once he learned who lived where, which he already knew anyway, there wouldn't be any problem.

His first day alone on the job he rode his truck through the fields, stopping now and again to get out and walk around, forgetting for a time that it was not enough simply to be in possession of the mail—that in order to be a mail carrier he had to deliver mail.

He stopped at one of the houses on his route. He put mail in the box. He liked the sound the metal latch made when he shut the lid. He opened it. He took the mail back out, put it back in his satchel, and drove off.

At two houses he forgot to stop.

At the Wilsons' he put the mail under a rock in the front flower bed.

Hello, said Noah.

Hello, said the Thompson family. They were sitting down to dinner, and Noah sat right down at the table with them. Mrs. Thompson had fried tenderloin and cooked a nice thick gravy, which Noah had smelled out on the front porch where two big dogs were whining and turning circles in front of the door.

I got your mail, said Noah, holding up the letters after he had eaten.

I can see that, Noah, Mr. Thompson said.

That, said Virgil later that afternoon, is not the correct way to carry the mail, or for that matter to do much of anything else. You pretending like you lost your spare parts again?

Noah smiled. He didn't answer. Instead, he thought about the way the white houses sat on slight eminences above the fields and were surrounded by barns and sheds and stock-filled pasture land. The way they were connected by roads that swept straight through the fields or ran short sweet curves through the remnants of oak and hickory forests. The way it felt riding along in the truck with his arm out the window, which had helped him remember the way it had felt, already years ago, riding along in the truck with his arm out the window, the warm, sweet air on their arms . . .

There were roses in the yards as he rode along with his mail sack, and there were daylilies in the side ditches. Daylilies meant there had once been a house or houses nearby. There had been so many houses. There had been their little house. The blue chicory meant nothing—it was just pretty to look at. The wind moved through the corn. There were long swaying shadows and clouds of yellow and white butterflies . . .

White butterflies, already years ago, on their driveway, and then, scattering them, a light rain. They had liked the rain, had loved to watch it from the front porch, or the kitchen window, splashing the red tulips, splattering the black dirt . . .

I have your mail.

I can see that.

I was married once. That is, I still am.

We know about it, Noah. And we're sorry.

We had a house once.

Well.

What's wrong with him?

He's all right, he gets spells sometimes. You feeling all right there, Noah? You want some water?

I'm feeling grand. I haven't felt better since my last birthday. I put the Wilson's mail under a rock by a lily.

I'll call over and tell them.

I got some extra here too.

That's Ethel Pritchard's and Lazarus Mitchell's. You better take it back on over there.

I will.

He did.

A few days later he got a call.

This is the United States Mail and we can not, said the Postmaster's assistant, have complaints.

Once upon a time, Noah had a job/Noah drove a truck/Noah saw lilies.

Once upon a time, Noah was happy/Noah lay down/Noah lay down not alone.

Once upon a time there were photographs on the Thompson's mantel beautiful photographs Noah stayed for dinner the boy in that photograph had died in a bunker in the war they told Noah there were photographs on the mantels of all the rooms that one had been in a charge and then had had to take cover in a bunker he had been a good boy everyone said so Noah nodded he remembered he smiled he lay down the dogs turned and turned on the front porch Noah got in his truck packed up the mail drove away and felt the warm air on his arm.

The messenger, said Virgil, after Noah had received the call from the Postmaster's assistant, is here (he made a small red mark).

The person/people/race to whom he/she/it is to deliver the message is/are here and say, here, he said (making two small blue marks).

The person/people/Deity/race who has/have sent for the messenger, who, that is, has/have the message that is to be, that must in fact be delivered is/are here, said Virgil (picking up a green pencil and walking off).

Is that a riddle?
Yes I think it is.

What's the answer?

I don't know I still haven't found any green mark.

Near the end of his life Noah asked Virgil if he had found the green mark and if he had could he please tell him where it was and Virgil looked at him for a long time then fell asleep then woke and looked at him then fell asleep again.

Dear Noah,

Yesterday, I got out of the bath. While I was in there all the leaves had fallen off the trees. I was sad when I saw they had already raked all the pretty leaves up. Part of the time in the bath it was cold and other times it was hot and I got burned some but mostly they gave me things and I just slept. What time is it there when you are reading this? Here, it is four o'clock. Today, they took us out riding in the bus. They drove us up a hill and they let us out to look around. The man who had built the hill was there and he said he would be happy to answer anyone's question about the hill. I asked him if he thought the hill could burn and he said he did not think so. He said it would be even nicer when it was covered with grass. Then, right there on the hill they had a show for us. There was some-one who juggled a little and a little girl who sang. There was some make-believe games, then they let us look at things and we drank lemonade, and I talked to the man again and he said, let's see, and set a match against the side of the hill.

Love, Opal

THE CAT IS NO LONGER SITTING on Noah's lap. It has gone off into one of the dark corners of the room where, every now and then, its eyes flash green or yellow. Noah has turned on the radio. It is a nice new portable with shiny buttons and dials that Max brought him. There is an all-night station out of Indianapolis that Noah likes. Sometimes there is music and other times talk. The voice that talks is deep and slow and often in the middle of this voice there are silences that fall through Noah's head like warm round stones. Every half hour there is a weather report. Noah has learned that the snow will stop by morning, and that tomorrow it will be clear. Clear, cold, and windy with some chance of drifting. Noah has always liked drifts. He likes it when the snow drifts over the fence rows, so that, when the snow hardens, he can walk right up and stand on top of the fence. Right now a woman is singing. It is an old recording and the voice sounds small and distant. When the song is finished there is a silence, then the deep voice says, beautiful, and Noah, who has been thinking about his mother, Ruby, standing at the front of the church, swaying slightly with her head held slightly back, and her hands at her sides, agrees. Noah is holding a pencil and a scrap of blue butcher paper. After a moment, he steadies the paper on his leg and begins to write. He writes. Slowly. Like he always does, like he has always done. Making each piece of each letter of his name: Noah Maximilien Summers. When he is finished, he surveys his work, decides it could do with a few flourishes, appends elaborate curlicues to some of the less finely wrought letters, sketches in a star or two, decides the result is satisfactory, then stands. There is another song playing. It is the same woman again. This time she is singing faster, and not so nicely, about a man who drinks then gets into his truck and drives away. The man stays gone for days, much the way Virgil did on several occasions before Noah was born.

In Virgil's case, the drinking and carrying on came after he had driven away, but his absences were prolonged and did weigh heavily, as the woman singing puts it, on Ruby's mind.

He'd get quiet and just drive off, Ruby would say later. Just up and leave—not even a good-bye. You know I had to do something.

What she did was 1) hire a private investigator from Kokomo who all but hauled Virgil back to the farm, 2) scream, 3) pray.

I don't rightly know why, said Virgil, when Noah asked him about it years later. I'd just get to where I didn't want to say a word, like I'd yapped myself out, like I'd shed my skin and had to find it again. Somehow that got wired in my mind with running around and whatnot.

You mean running around with ill-reputed ladies and colorful individuals?

I'm not answering you on that one.

That Virgil's absences were connected to his bouts of silence made perfect sense to Noah, the connection seeming to be one of both degree and kind. Noah's certainty about the bi-part nature of the connection wasn't confirmed, however, until death came to cap Virgil's later years of silence, and the Minister, subsequent to delivering the briefest of eulogies, remarked to Noah on that "aggravated permanent absence born of the dubious, oh-how-dubious glory that was your father's."

Noah has often thought that his own incipient absence must, by the Minister's logic, be of a similarly aggravated nature, although he was never, like Virgil, found in a hotel room playing cards with one man and two women wearing feathered boas and little else and upward of a gallon of gin, and never, thoughts excluded, called the Minister, or any Minister, "dumber than a jackrabbit and uglier than a head-beat pig."

Still, Noah counts his own prospects for glory as dubious to say the least, and although he long ago stopped going to church, the thought bothers him.

Not long after Noah had lost his job carrying the mail, and they were walking through waist-high timothy discussing what Virgil, without smiling, called his "earlier escapades," Virgil told Noah he wished regret didn't last any longer than the beads of liquid they'd just done such a fine job of sponging up into their shoes and pants, but that it did last longer, much longer, forever even. Noah believes this. He also believes what he recently heard someone say on television, that regret resulting from inaction, or, even worse, from ineffective action, could be greater than that caused by what one had done.

Ineffective and aggravated action, thinks Noah. He looks at his name on the piece of butcher paper, steadies himself on the back of the chair, then winds his way slowly across the cluttered room. In the center of the west wall, between a collapsing pie safe and an icebox, sits a pale yellow dresser with three large drawers. The bottom and top drawers are filled with old magazines and seed catalogues. In the center drawer, on the remains of one of Ruby's old bolts of red cloth, sits a second, slightly smaller mask, Opal's. Noah touches it—a pretty face with high cheekbones and a large lovely mouth—then places the scrap of butcher paper beside it on the red cloth and, without closing the drawer, walks back over to the stove.

For many years, Noah saw things, all kinds of things, had visions, dreamed things while he was awake. Now, if he sees anything worth mentioning, he generally sees it, like most people, when he is asleep, but for a long time when he was wide awake interesting things would appear. Once, out in the south field, for example, Noah saw a clock. He did not ask Virgil, who was driving the tractor, if he could see it—he knew he couldn't—but he did ask him to stop.

What is it?

A clock.

What kind of clock?

It's tall. Old looking. Flowers carved into it. It's got one of them things. It's moving back and forth.

A pendulum.

Must be.

You say it's moving back and forth?

Virgil stopped the tractor and Noah jumped off and walked over to the clock, which Virgil could not see and which, Noah told him, was standing taller than either of them at the edge of the field.

It's ticking, said Noah.

Virgil nodded. Virgil smiled. What time does it say?

Noah had seen other things out in the fields before. Once he saw an old man in deer skins holding an antler in one hand and in the other a geode that had been cracked open so that the jagged lavender interior gleamed in the Sun. Once he saw a log cabin that, Virgil learned later, had been knocked down seventy-five years before, and went inside and sat down by a fire, and Virgil saw him talking to himself and sitting cross-legged on the ground. Once, he saw nothing, plain nothing, the fields, the fence rows, the far-off sky had just vanished, and once he saw what afterwards he shuddered a little at the thought of and called strange thicknesses in the air.

This time, when the clock vanished, Noah got a stick and began turning the packed earth along the edge of the field, exposing a coal-black loamy soil that was, said Virgil, "all breaded up with oak fibers" and teeming with worms. After a moment, Noah hit the edge of something. He put his hand into the earth and pulled out the almost completely rusted remains of what turned out to be the face from Noah's great-grandmother's pendulum clock.

It used to sit right there, said Ruby that evening after Noah had sponged all the dirt off what was left of the face then set it on the kitchen table, and Virgil had dumped a pocketful of dirt and wood fiber and crumbling cogs and springs onto a napkin (none of which, with the exception of the dirt, and that only later, Ruby showed any inclination to touch) and the two of them had followed her into the front hall and she had stood facing the empty corner and pointed.

It sat catty-corner, she said. We used to lose balls and such behind it and had to ask permission to fetch them. Your great-grandmother kept the key in her apron pocket and every night she'd give it a turn. I don't think it was what you would call a pretty clock. I'm not sure that the wood was even finished. But it kept time and your great-grandmother used to sit in a chair over there and watch it. It made a funny noise at the quarter hour and you could see the pendulum going back and forth and when we got sleepy we used to sit with her and look at our-selves in the glass door until we got sent up to bed.

Ruby stopped speaking and Noah looked at her then the three of them stood looking at the corner. There was a crack in the white paint where the walls came together. Noah waited for Ruby to speak, to say whatever else there was to say, but she did not say it and instead sent them back into the kitchen to "get that mess off my table," which the two of them did, each collecting his own part of it, Ruby lingering a moment longer by the corner in the front hall.

The next day Noah and Virgil filled three tubs with the soil that had surrounded the clock. The geraniums Ruby planted in them grew enormous and lived for over twenty years, prompting Virgil to comment, standing in front of one of them much later, on the "temporal fecundity" of the earth the tubs had contained (an earth that even Ruby had allowed, upon inspection that very evening after they had found it, looked "rich enough to bake"). Whenever Virgil made reference to the anecdote afterwards, he never neglected to mention that one of the fish they caught the following weekend with a worm pulled from the dirt was big enough to be measured and bragged about, without exaggeration, in the parking lot after church.

It wasn't until a week after they had found it that Noah, who had just affixed the rusted face to his bedroom wall and was lying on his bed watching the light advance slowly across the floor, realized that he did in fact already know the story of the clock, that Ruby had long before told it to him as if it were something that had happened elsewhere, to others, though she had never, and she now declined to discuss it (all right I'll tell you, said Virgil), mentioned it again.

THERE ONCE WAS AN OLD WOMAN, your great-grandmother, who lived in a house with a family (her own and now your own) that had been very much and very tragically reduced. That reduction had taken place during and just after that part of what she was afterwards known to call, by turns, "That Miserable Little War," or "That Impossible Idiocy Against the Indians," which had, when the second major part of the family reduction occurred, been trickled out to pretty much just one side of the men in the war dying, and then pretty much just one side of the women and children dying one way or another as a result of the circumstance of that pretty much one side of men. Is that clear?

No.

I just mean that by that time it was mainly just the Indians doing the dying.

Why?

Guns and numbers. Trickery. I don't know. May I continue?

Yes.

Well, despite the fact that it was mainly just the Indians doing the dying, a man from the other side, our side, I suppose, did die. Then a woman from the other side died. The man had been in the Dakotas and Wyoming and Montana and Colorado. Where he died was in Kentucky. Although almost across the border back into Indiana—a wagon had been arranged to haul the tubercular man home. But, as I say, a man died and shortly thereafter a woman died, and so they were dead and your great-grandmother, who had waited four years for his return and twelve weeks longer for their return, instead received a letter from the United States Government followed two days later (he had been a popular captain, she a popular captain's wife) by their flag-wrapped remains. That evening she had asked the hired man to fetch her the light axe, and had set to work.

She told your mother that she had meant the gesture to indi-
cate her desire to lose or kill time, or both, but that time, even
if you had fabricated the most intricate symbolic unrender-
ings of it, could neither be killed nor lost. But then think if it
could. (Noah had tried.) Just think. (He had not been able.)
What impossible series of adjustments would you have to make,
to recorrespond yourself, if it recombobulated itself, or if you
ever found it again?

Something dark, something liquid—a dome. Who were all those people?

Your mother's people. Which ones?

I told you. Your great-grandmother, the one who chopped up the clock. Your grandfather—your great-grandmother's son, the one who fought in the Indian wars and died. Your grandmother, the one who went to Kentucky to bring your grandfather home and died in her turn.

What about my great-grandfather?

He was the circuit rider. He'd died some years before. Why flag-wrapped?

I just explained that. Because he was a war hero and he died. They wrap them up in flags.

Is that true?

I'm not certain.

And she was a war hero's wife?

Yes.

What is a war hero?

You're too old for that kind of question. Someone who fights well and bravely. In a war. Or someone who people decide has fought well and bravely. Hector. Agamemnon. Nelson. Lafayette. Little Turtle. Crazy Horse. Joan of Arc. Ulysses S. Grant.

Why am I too old?

Never mind.

Did Grandfather fight well and bravely?

I don't know. Most likely. Though it was mostly against people who couldn't fight back.

What did he look like?

I don't know.

What did Grandmother look like?

You know what she looked like, there's pictures in the album.

How did she die?

T.B.

Were they really afraid to go out playing in the fields afterwards—after Great-Grandma took her axe to that clock?

Who told you that?

Ruby.

Don't call your mother that.

Sorry.

Anyway, I don't know. You'll have to ask her.

Noah did. That night. She was halfway up the stairs to bed, and she answered without stopping, her voice rising up into the house away from him,

Yes

Noah followed her. His feet making the boards creak in the same places as hers—fourth and seventh and eleventh steps.

Mother, said Noah, how many wars have there been Mother? he said, or he said something else, probably something else, Should I be afraid? or, Were you afraid? (anything to elicit another ascending affirmative—in recent years, in hopes of hearing some echo, he has taken to flinging his own cracked voice up the empty staircase: Yes, he says, Yes, Yes) but she didn't answer, didn't stop. The eleventh step creaked under Noah's right foot, but she had already disappeared into her room.

How many wars have there been, Daddy? said Noah, later, after he had come back down the stairs.

They were sitting in front of the fireplace. Virgil reading aloud. Noah listening. Both of them facing the fire, the painting of deep blue cornflowers, the small clock.

Noah repeated his question.

I don't know.

Noah suggested a number. Virgil shrugged.

And how many great-grandmothers have chopped up and buried clocks?

In that war?

In any war.

Thousands.

Dear Noah,

How I hope that all is going well for you. Yesterday, they brought in a gal who said she was carrying nine babies and couldn't stop asking what she was going to do. I tried to imagine what it would be like to have nine in there but couldn't get past one. It is five days now since they have given me the electricity. Instead I am to play with heavy balls and to work in the dairy and think pretty thoughts. Fire is not a pretty thought. Curtains are a pretty thought. Fire and curtains together are not a pretty thought. Pretty curtains are a pretty thought. Pretty is a pretty thought. Dinner is a pretty thought. Nine babies is too many. One is too many. No, it's not. I'm sorry, Noah. It is late now and there is no dinner. They are having shortages. Send me up something again if you think about it. I liked that pudding cake. I wouldn't mind some of those little sausages. The ones with the nice sauce in the pretty tins.

Love, Opal

NOAH HAS PLUGGED in the Christmas lights. They hang in a double string above the tool bench. Max found them in a moldering cardboard box and rigged them up soon after he arrived. Noah can see the beads of bright color blinking slowly on and off in the Egyptian cat's slowly blinking eyes. Egypt, thinks Noah, looking at the old broken-eared Indiana farm cat and thinking of the huge, slow curves he once saw on a television program about the Nile. In the program, scientists were trying to determine how, using primitive boats, it had been possible to transport obelisks to sites far downriver. They could understand how the boats, once the obelisk had been loaded, could move down the river—this was difficult to imagine, but conceivable. They could not, however, understand how the ancient Egyptians had loaded the long, almost impossibly heavy stones, without capsizing the boats. Noah decides he will ask Max what he thinks about this. Max will probably have an answer. He is pretty good with answers. Virgil would definitely have had an answer. Or would have made one up. The Christmas lights come on. The cat blinks and when its eyes open again the lights are gone, and, at that moment, Noah reaches over and unplugs them. The Romans, Noah remembers Virgil saying, believed that some aspect of everything they saw dissolved into atoms and entered their bodies through the eyes, engendering, Virgil had paused to conjecture, an almost constant rearranging of the brain. The Romans believed it was when two people saw each other simultaneously, and their respective atoms mingled in midflight, sliding one past the other and circling, slowly, back and forth, before entry into the eye sockets, that love was ignited, and the two people proceeded to comport themselves as if "lost in a dazzling mist."

Can cows fall in love?

I don't know, it's just a story.

How about pigs?

Virgil smiled and Noah smiled then Noah fell in love and pretty soon they both stopped smiling, and now Noah pictures himself standing alone and smiling in the middle of the desert, a sandstorm rising and the air around him filling with the finest rock. Or with the finest ice. Max says it's a wonder the air doesn't freeze solid. He says that at any given moment the air over Indiana is filled with millions of gallons of vaporized water. For that matter it's a wonder, says Max (smiling), we don't all drown. Noah almost drowned. He was ice fishing with a church group on a lake in the northern part of the county and, at the exact moment the rod jumped, the ice below Noah's stool cracked. When they pulled him out he was still holding onto the rod and when they reeled in the line out of the water came a four-pound smallmouth bass. Afterwards, as he lay in bed recovering from what had quickly become pneumonia, Noah would lie with his eyes closed listening to his own labored breathing and to the familiar sounds of the house and farm around him, and wonder what it might be like to live those winter months below the ice in such gloom. Like nothing at all.

Like nothing at all is right, Ruby said when two weeks after the incident he wondered this aloud. Whoever filled your head with that kind of foolish thought?

Noah said he didn't know, and Ruby said well in any case it probably wouldn't hurt to say his prayers, which he did, repeating over and over, in what the doctor later called a state of fever-induced delirium, first, I will be a fisherman for Christ, then, after a few minutes, I will be a fish for Christ, then, simply, though screaming it, I will be a fish.

Are you finished now, Mr. Fish? said Virgil, who Noah's yelling had brought in from where he was reshoeing one of the horses in the back barn lot. Noah didn't know and still doesn't know but is beginning to suspect he is. He imagines he sees himself out of the cat's eyes and that what he the cat sees is nothing more than something that still emits a little heat and still occasionally moves.

Cat, says Noah. Do I look anything like a fish to you? he says. He smiles. Barely. The cat watches him. It lifts a paw and licks it. Noah shot a cat once. An old black tom that was killing all the new kittens, tearing them into pieces that it left strewn across the greenhouse.

Noah caught it one afternoon coming across the yard. He put a bullet in its back haunches, and it leapt five feet straight up into the air and, before he could reload, disappeared. A few weeks later, when he was tearing down Ruby's old potting shed, he found its carcass in the space under the floorboards. The eyes were gone and the worms and silverfish were at it. Noah knelt by the old criminal for a time then went and got the shovel and dug a hole for it. He has not used the rifle since.

Well, cat, says Noah looking at the cat that is alive and thinking of the cat that is dead. Are you alive right now, right this second, or are you dead? asks Noah. The cat looks up at Noah, raises itself up on its haunches, and butts its head against his chin. Sorry, that was a fool question, Noah says. Noah puts his arm around the cat's lean flank and pulls it close to him. He likes this cat very much and wonders if he should ask Max to build a small pyramid for it. Just a small one. For when it goes. Like Egypt. Max could call and have them bring a load of sand.

Dear Noah,

Remember the time you said you had met a man coming out of the corn without a face as you were on the way back from Hillisburg? I like that the man said, when you asked him, that his name was "You." I liked that he didn't have a face, or one you didn't know how to see. Well, You, just a minute ago I met someone funny too. Instead of the doctor I went into the office and found a ventriloquist, who was making cardboard children tell ghost stories. Every few minutes all but one of the cardboard children coughed. Then I coughed. Then I was sitting down next to the ventriloquist on the ventriloquist's bed. Watch, I said. But I knew I hadn't actually said anything because I didn't know what it was we were going to watch. Neither did she. That is the end, You. That is the end.

Love, Opal

NOAH IS DREAMING. A moment ago he dreamed that he was rolled up tight in a bolt of chilled black cloth that was slowly drying and tightening as it did so, but now the dream has shifted. In the center of the new dream sits a box with a hole in its side. Noah, happy to have the use of his arms again, lifts the box and places the hole against his eye. Inside the box the Sun is shining. The ground is covered with snow and there are several trees with black trunks and there is a blue sky. Noah waits with his eye against the hole. Soon he can see a small piece of color moving off in the distance. It moves quickly, darting from trunk to trunk, coming nearer. A male cardinal. It swoops down across the snow then up onto a tree. Back and forth it goes. The red feathers shine against the black trunks. Noah wants to say something. Anything. Cardinal, he wants to say, or Minister or Bishop or King, but he can't speak, only his eye is in the box.

Noah has had other dreams like this one. Usually they involve at least a partial abrogation of the senses: either he can only see or only hear or, more rarely and not for many years, can only speak. In that dream he would invariably be in the presence of ten or twelve elders who sat invisibly waiting. And, just like when at family events his mind had gone blank at his turn to recite or sing, so now in this "speaking" dream, Noah felt his lungs and vocal cords hovering above a wordlessness that could not, even in the sternly expectant half presence of those elders, be revoked. He could, however, produce sound, which with a sense of great urgency he did—more than once Virgil or Ruby woke him to stop his "babbling and yelling" and "thrashing around." Finally, though Virgil did not approve and would not stay to greet him, the Minister was consulted. Ruby said she couldn't know and did not wish to presume but thought the Lord must be involved in the situation, and the Minister listened with great attention then stood, touched Noah on the shoulder, and said,

It's nothing. Go in peace. The Lord sayeth, "Ye shall dream of Heaven," and you shall.

Almost immediately his "babbling" dreams stopped. Noah associated their cessation not so much with what the Minister had said, but with the Minister's imposing forehead and long arms and strong smell. Nevertheless, for weeks afterwards on Sunday afternoons as they sat on the back porch for dinners of pork chops or stuffed peppers or ham and beans with cucumbers and onions or ham loaf scalloped potatoes tenderloin or fried chicken and gravy or Swiss steak and gravy or okra carrot and cabbage salad squash or pumpkin blossoms, Noah's favorite, they were fried in flour and oil, Ruby directed conversation about the morning's sermon, sometimes sending Noah into the living room to fetch her Bible, from which Virgil, though not passionately, would read. Noah cannot remember which passages Virgil read, but can remember his own passage, from dinner table to Ruby's large white double-handled handbag, and then the passage, blue then green then red carpet, back through the gently creaking house. One of his parents, either Virgil for Ruby or Ruby for herself, had hung a stained-glass cardinal above the jade plant in the south window of the dining room, and one Sunday, just as he had stepped slowly from living room into dining room, a tight grouping of rays shooting down through the crab apple tree outside transfixed the crimson glass and cut across the top of the jade plant to lie in flecks across the book and make (he had stopped short) a vague red half circle at the base of his left thumb. When, a few minutes later, his parents asked him what had happened, he told them he had seen himself as a baby floating in the air above the dining room table, and that the baby had been livid and stone silent and that the walls had been shimmering and that after that he had fallen down.

Late one night during this period, Noah stopped outside his parents' room on the way to the toilet. There was a bar of light at the bottom of their door and up out of this bar of light came Virgil's voice, amused but also slightly outraged, saying, You don't really mean to tell me you think when he was having his nightmares and such he was up there? Since there in Noah's mind was a suffocating urge to speak without the prospect of ever again having any access to words, Noah bent to the bar of light and whispered,

no

a simple negation that Noah, dreaming all these years later, finds himself wishing his lidless eye could insert into the light-filled box, and wondering what the word "no," inserted into such fragile circumstances, would do to the cardinal, the snow, the tall black trunks. Soon, as if in partial answer, the dream, like everything else in Noah's life, has shifted again, the scene has been erased, and Noah finds himself sitting on top of one of the corn bins looking down and out over a bean field intermittently lit by thousands of fireflies, which make of its lush, dark surface a strange, inexplicably liquid, plain of stars.

Dear Noah,

I was bored then a woman came and gave a presentation on those Indian dirt mounds we have here in our wonderful old Indiana. Did you know that Indiana had a Trail of Death, dear Noah? We marched those Indians out of here, out of good old Indiana, and a lot of them died. The woman called that our ugly history. That's what I call it too. She said if you dig in the dirt mounds like she did you found shells and hatchets and pottery and pretty stones. She said you found beads and bowls and knife blades and bones curled up like they were babies sleeping. She said you found fire pits and animal skulls and figurines and sundry charred articles. She said that by looking at the articles and the layers of dirt that both supported and covered them you could figure things out about the people who lived there, what they wore and thought and such. Isn't that a lovely idea? I asked her if the dirt was warm. She said it was surprisingly warm. All day since I've been thinking. They told me I had to quit but I didn't quit. I'll never quit. I've been putting the blanket over my head and curling up and closing my eyes.

Love, Opal

NOAH HAS SLEPT and now he is standing at the window looking out through a line he has rubbed along the cold, frost-covered glass. It is a short, thick line just long and wide enough for Noah's eyes and looking out through it makes Noah feel, for a moment, as though he has already slipped on the mask. Outside, the wind is still blowing across the snow and now and then it lifts a small frozen cloud and carries it spinning through the yellow haze of the service lamp. At the edge of the light, half-buried in snow, is a 1948 Cub tractor that has not moved from where it sits since its engine blew up under Virgil in 1963. In the summer, timothy, Queen Anne's lace, goldenrod, and morning glories grow up around the collapsing tractor, and one sun-glazed afternoon last August as they were walking past it, Max said, looks like you have grown yourself a burning bush. Once or twice after Max said this, just on the off chance, Noah went out in the afternoon and stood by it, but he saw nothing. Just the old tractor. Steaming in the yard. And Virgil climbing down off it to come sit by Noah on a stump.

I WAS TRAINED as a schoolteacher, which, as you know, is how I met your mother, she sat in the first row, and even if a lot like you she couldn't get reading and writing down too well she led us all when it was time to discuss or sing. But at any rate I did not belong here at first or perhaps ever but I'd already made a fool out of myself bragging to your great-grandmother's hired men that I could plow a field as well as anyone out of the Old Testament and that meant better than any one of them and being put to prove it and getting dragged right back into the barn plow and all by those horses and for the rest of the day all of them raising their hands and saying Sir and asking to use the facility and then me suggesting to one of them that I might lay the back of my teacher's hand across his face and them finding that funny too and my not at least not right that instant finding that funny and getting near-whipped for it just as the supper bell was ringing and then without even getting up off the grass declaiming Ronsard then reciting the fall of Hector to them and then explaining it and then reciting some of it again and then after that though I reckon there is more to it and likely even much more I guess it will be sufficient to say, whatever my subsequent failings and transgressions, that I might have done near upon anything to be involved with that mother of yours.

NOAH, LOOKING OUT THROUGH THE LINE, which is just frosting over again, sees Virgil coming slowly across the corner of the yard on the red tractor, the tractor engine steaming, then a bang and the tractor, forever, stopped, and Virgil climbing down off of it.

What's wrong with it now?
    It's broke.
    You going to fix it?
    I'm done fixing.
    What do you mean?
    I mean I'm done. I'm going. Good-bye. Adieu. Adios. Au revoir.

THERE ARE OTHER THINGS IN THE YARD. Invisible now. Out at the edge of the garden beyond the light, for example, sits an old washing machine. Noah cannot clearly remember how or why the washing machine, which used to sit in the basement, came to be where it is, but all spring and summer as he works in the garden the machine is there, and often as he passes by he hits the hollow metal top with his hand. The sound goes out to the edges of the garden and stops. Sometimes a bird rises. Or a cat is startled. Sometimes, he startles himself. The washing machine has only rusted in one or two spots, and Noah likes to see the white enamel glistening after a rain or gleaming in the moonlight. Every now and then, when the weather permits, and he is feeling, as he puts it to himself, a little more foolish than ordinary, he carries a stool out and sits down in front of the machine and looks into the dark, rusted interior through the cracked glass covering the door.

One night, near the end of her life, Ruby came slowly down the basement steps and found him in a similar position, sitting on a stool, his face lit by the illuminated dial, the machine, gently churning, empty of all but warm water and soap. She stood beside him, holding a hand on his shoulder, her breathing quick and shallow, her reflection joining his in a circle around the edges of the glass door.

What are you doing?

Nothing.

Ruby nodded.

I suppose you're cleaning the inside of that thing.

Noah didn't answer.

Well it probably needs it.

They watched the water move. It rose and fell and slopped soap against the glass.

You seeing anything special?

Noah could see things but it didn't matter. He told Ruby it didn't matter. He could see, even though it didn't matter, the church basement full of people on a Sunday evening. Lines of light were coming into the room through the half-windows. It was the yearly Ham Supper. The older women of the church stood in a row with shining spoons and aprons. The men and younger women and children came past carrying plates that the older women filled with food then they sat and the Minister a Minister Noah didn't know said grace all he said was the word grace and that was all they started eating everything was fine except that little bits of the people were burning and even that was fine little bits so they didn't notice but Noah noticed they kept eating and talking and following the supper children sang one of them with a small beautiful voice it reminded Noah of a wren and out of the arms and necks and shoulders of all of them rose the bright nickels of flame.

Noah told Ruby it didn't matter. He told Ruby he had never seen anything when it might have helped to see anything so it didn't matter.

You helped the Sheriff those times.

That's been a while, a long while.

Still.

Noah shook his head.

It does matter, Ruby said, taking her hand off his shoulder.

It does, she said.

She said it once more as she was walking away from him and Noah watched her reflection race around the incurved edges of the door. For a moment it mixed with his and the moment after that it was gone.

Why does it matter? Noah asked.

Ruby paused at the foot of the stairs beside one of the empty plant benches and said, your father was the one had all the answers, I reckon pretty soon we'll have to carry those jade plants in.

Noah nodded. He knew she had not seen him nod. He had seen himself nod. She walked slowly back up the red steps and two days later he was sprinkling corn around her bed.

COULD I SING? Your great-grandmother said I was born with a canary in my throat. She used to have me stand next to her and sing "Amazing Grace." She'd hum, I'd sing. After her it was the Minister who first really noticed. That was our Minister at Hill's Baptist, Reverend Stokes. It was a children's choir. We were singing "The Old Wooden Cross." Mildred Little was playing the piano and just like that Reverend Stokes said, stop. So Mildred stopped. So did we. Then the Reverend told me to step forward. I want everyone else to just listen now, he said. Then he nodded to Mildred and she started playing "Let There Be Peace on Earth," and Reverend Stokes said, now Ruby. Now Ruby, I want you to take another step forward and sing.

ON THE OTHER SIDE OF THE GARDEN, standing between the hog sheds, is a refrigerator, and directly behind that is a wood-burning oven in which Ruby once baked pies. Near the house stands a half-dead cherry tree that they used to cover with pieces of black net to keep the birds off.

blue jay cardinal yellow finch crow
in French those are what we call oiseaux

That's what your father used to call them. He used to sing that. Before we were married. Wazo.

That's right, said Virgil.

They were standing in the yard holding pieces of net. L'oiseau se perche dans l'arbre, said Virgil. Il mange les cérises. Ce n'est pas bien. Il ne faut pas que l'oiseau mange les cérises.

What's a wazo? said Noah.

Oiseau, said Virgil. I'm trying to tell you. Without an x at the end it's singular. That means there's just one of them. Without an s in the middle it's all vowels. All the vowels.

Noah tried saying it. He said it. Wazo.

A oiseau landed and stuck its beak in a cherry. Virgil said, Partez!

Noah said, Wazo.

Ruby said, It's not a wazo when it's eating my cherries. It's just a plain old jay.

The three of them took turns climbing the ladder up through the small, cool leaves and plucking big, fat cherries by the bucketful, but most of the time, because she intended to make pies with them and required "just the right ones," it was Ruby. Noah can see her, brow slightly furrowed, carrying the bucket across the yard, then standing by the window in the pantry, her wrists and forearms covered with flour, her hands in a large white bowl, and he can hear her saying

the secret to dough is it has to rest

Like God, a very young Noah pronounced with great solemnity one Sunday dinner after Ruby had, with almost palpable satisfaction, repeated what had become known as her litany, in response to a particularly delicate crust that had, by more than one person, been favorably commented upon.

Why that's right, Aunt Sylvie had said before being joined in a table-wide burst of laughter, a laughter that sounded, to Noah, a little like fresh hard rain.

They also laughed, though differently, a little less comfortably, at what Noah said next.

No, said Ruby.

Why? said Virgil, an interested smile on his face. Why do you say God is like that?

Because he's like dough.

Why because he's like dough?

Because dough goes in the oven like the Devil and cooks.

Later, when the others had left and Noah sat on his small chair in the corner watching Ruby wash and dry, he asked her why God had rested when down here there was still always so much work.

He didn't really rest, said Ruby. He didn't rest like we do. He didn't sleep.

Does dough rest like we do? Noah asked.

I don't know. That's a silly question, Noah.

How do we rest?

By sleeping. By sitting still.
By dreaming?
I don't know.
Does God dream?
I reckon he must.
Does the Devil rest?
Ruby didn't answer.
Am I resting now?
No, you are not sitting still.

For years Ruby baked two pies a day, once wondering aloud how many orchards worth of fruit she had picked. Virgil, sitting in his chair by the window had answered, smiling,

> I think about a thousand

and Noah, leaning against the counter, had looked up and seen a forest of fruit trees sprout up and spread out across the kitchen, spill into the walls, into his parents, dark and glowing like a color illustration from *The Arabian Nights*.

Not long afterwards, Noah rounded a corner and came face to face with an oversize photograph of Virgil swaying gently, as if blown by breezes, beside the daybed in the front hall. As Noah watched, the room around him began to fill with photographs of angels eating photographs of pie with perfect crust. When he looked he saw there were photographs of clocks hung around each of the angels' necks. A photograph of Ruby was there for a moment. And one of Opal. Both of them were wearing photographs of clocks. There was no photograph of a clock, however, hung around Virgil's neck.

I lost time
and could not find it again

the gently swaying photograph of Virgil wearing his fishing
hat and holding his fishing pole said.

Noah hasn't. It surrounds him.

There are moments when he can hear it,

quite clearly ticking,

as if the fields were preparing to explode.

SOMETIMES, AS HE SITS IN THE SHED, as he does now, Noah closes his eyes and listens, and, after a moment, though he has not stopped listening, the sounds of the shed, of the surrounding night, of his own faint, rough breathing fall far away, and every sound he hears is remembered.

rain

rain like cold ropes

rain in late winter cold

rain

Or spring. Spring and the rain falling

was rain they wanted and they would stop what they were doing every now and again and say,

listen

Noah would listen

And in the summer it was the sound of oaks splitting, as if someone or something had grabbed one apart and left his ears and arms and teeth hurting. And the rain beat the leaves and slammed into the ground then stopped or did not stop but softened, so that the sound was round, then started again, hard again, and another oak split or enormous cannon shot or a vein of onyx air was ripped open, and someone in the house would wonder whether or not there would be hail. Then there was hail, and it was either small or it was not and either way he could hear it hitting off the roof and knew then that it must be hitting into the corn, Virgil's hands would start tapping on the edges of the armrests if he was sitting, which is the way Noah remembers it, whenever it hailed—Virgil in the armchair next to the radio and Ruby by the window, always by the window, and Virgil watching her out of the corner of his eyes, tapping on the orange armrests, and Noah watching both of them, and then Ruby said,

it's stopped.

And it had stopped and when they went outside the sky was blue and the yard was white and Ruby could now talk about what she had been thinking about while she looked out the window

one of those books with pictures
I want one of them

one of those books with little pictures where the sky is open and God is there with a dove

and there is white manna covering the ground

she could talk about this because while the yard was white, the garden and the fields were still a deep, rich green or whatever color they were supposed to be after a deep, rich rain, and Virgil could say,

we will find that book

and to Noah,

try some

and Noah scooped up a handful of icy gravel-sized pellets and did.

Or it was autumn, late autumn, and the rain had been coming down for hours, and the grass and the yellow leaves on the grass and the small brown leaves that had blown off the hickory and onto the garden and the earth, the freshly plowed earth, and all of it, especially Noah as he went into the house or left the house and went into the barn where the cows stood steaming, was cold, Noah was cold as he carried something for Ruby across the yard, and he was cold as he carried something for Virgil across the wet garden, Noah's hands freshly bandaged, Noah looking back over his shoulder at something and seeing his tracks and the brown leaves he had mashed and then looking up and seeing Virgil and Virgil not smiling at him looking hard at him as if in that instant something had come up out of the earth and stuffed him full of cold leaves and smashed rock and sour liquid. Virgil much more in that moment than merely Noah's father—something enormous something quietly enraged, an embodiment of the cold, the rain, the miles of rough dark acreage around them. Noah wanting to wrap his ruined hands around all of it, Virgil most of all, and squeeze

Noah looking over his shoulder then turning and continuing

on across the cemetery where Virgil and Ruby were buried the stones all around theirs yawed and Noah yawed a little as he stood first ruined hands in pockets then ruined hands removed from pockets to cover his face or almost cover his face then his eyes open and his ruined hands at his sides and the rain raining cold and the freshly turned earth turned freshly for one then for the other then for Opal only that was in another cemetery and when he looked up there was no rain it was early winter this winter and in place of the rain there were stars and wind then cold wind and snow.

Snow, deep and drifting, brings Noah back to the shed again. He crosses his arms over his chest, stretches his legs, and sees that Virgil—his most frequent visitor—has left the grave in his head and is standing on the other side of the room staring at him. He stares and stares, and Noah stares back and thinks, I'm tired, then thinks what he has thought before around this time of night, I reckon now I've reached the deepest hours in which men and women and chickens drown.

Hello Virgil, he says, eventually. You here to tell me you found time? That you got it figured out? That you found that green mark?

Virgil's mouth opens and begins moving, and as it does the rest of him resolves itself into darkness once more, so that for a moment there is just the mouth, wide lips and large teeth, moving soundlessly. Then the mouth, which strikes Noah as a tiny, almost pathetic thing without its face, without the words it seems intent on shaping, stops moving and vanishes too. And when it does, as if they had been trailing along in its wake, the words arrive: dreams again, riddles, half stories, the whole joined by other voices, threads of memory, shreds of an incomplete pattern distilled in the Indiana night and poured from a pitcher of cold air into Noah's head.

HERE IS A DREAM. In going somewhere from somewhere else, which by the way is the oldest story, my companion and I are set the labor of transporting a recently dead woman to some destination along the way. She is stiff and very light. I take the feet and my companion the head and the neck. And so we walk. Then it has changed and we are tired and the dead woman is walking beside us to make it easier. After a while she climbs back onto our hands, which are still held as if we had never stopped holding her. At some point she divides herself into neat segments for us to carry. She says to me, Virgil you look tired, give Noah the heavy parts. I do, and we continue on along the road. The two of us. You and me. Although I guess it's really three of us. Maybe more. I can't tell anymore. We walk along and don't say anything. On and on.

HERE IS ANOTHER. Once upon a time there was a farmer who one night had this dream and the next morning fell into a folly. The dream was this: He was walking, blind-folded and waist-deep, in his own field, through a channel of smooth, rich, powder-soft dirt which gave less resistance against his legs than water. He walked and walked, follow-ing that channel and wondering where he could be going because the channel kept requiring him to curve and turn and sometimes even go back on himself. He walked, as I say, and walked and sometimes he was sure he was where he had already been and sometimes he was tortured by the thought that he wasn't and sometimes, not so very far off in the distance, he heard soft, muttering voices, that sounded to him, when he thought about it, much like his own. And then he woke. And that might have been the end of it, one strange dream among others, except that in his passage that morn-ing from bed to bathroom he walked, as it occurred, between two mirrors, one hung opposite the other, one of them new and having been hung there—a hook being available—out of convenience, the previous afternoon, so that in one mirror was the image of the other, and in the other, the image of the one, and in that one, also, its own image, as in the other, and so on, so that the farmer, who was still to some degree step-ping through the soft cool dirt of his dream, and now found himself strung between the two mirrors, and the effect they created of his repeated image being pulled away from him and into the walls, felt himself caught, stopped, he said after-wards, somewhere between dismay and delight, so that when his wife stirred, almost an hour later, woken, she said after-wards, by the sound of the cows complaining, "That was how I found him, that was how I found him," she said.

AT THE END, when your father wasn't talking at all anymore and he got so he would wander, though of course not like what he used to, I got worried. I got so I would hide things. You know better than any how many ways there are to get hurt or to hurt yourself on a farm and I've never known a farm to have as many sharp edges as this one. There were times when you weren't around and I had to get out that I would lock him in the bedroom, but he didn't like that, you could tell. More often though, I'd leave him those notes in his pockets. I got Lois Wilson to write them so they'd be clear: Don't lean your forehead against the glass in the bathroom. Don't stand on the road. Come home now. I love you. Don't go looking for dead squirrels in the ditches. Ask Noah. Use the facility if you got business. The Lord *is* your shepherd, you listen to Him.

NOAH FOUND HIM ONCE. In the middle of the night. He was, in fact, standing in the bathtub with his forehead pressed lightly against the window-glass, and when Noah came in and spoke to him he made no move, and, after a minute, Noah went right ahead and used the toilet. Ten minutes later he returned, and Virgil was still there, and Noah came up behind him and took him gently by the shoulders and pulled him back. Sitting on the white windowsill in front of him were a shell, some dirt, and a small rusted spring. Noah could feel Virgil breathing. He could feel himself breathing. He could see the back of Virgil's neck, pale and deeply wrinkled and soft looking in the dim light. Why? Noah whispered into the neck. The neck did not answer. It looked, however, as if given time it might make some answer, and so Noah waited, holding his father by the shoulders, gently by the shoulders and looking into the neck, until, after a time, the neck did answer, or rather seemed to answer, for although it spoke to Noah, although Noah could quite clearly hear it, he had no idea what it said.

THERE ARE ALL KINDS of holidays or holy days or whatever you care to call them and each carries with it its own accretions of meanings and for each one of us those accretions are slightly different. Take an example. We, that's my brother, your Uncle Johnson, and myself, were up at Ginny Smith's for a tree trimming a few days before Christmas must have been 1886. It had been clear and we'd spent the morning sliding and throwing rocks at the creek then the sky changed fast and we went inside and the lamps had been lit and we looked out the window at the clouds. Then it started snowing. It snowed and we sat at the windows and watched it and when the windows froze over we rubbed pictures in them and then we left the windows to string popcorn and berries and sing songs. They had colored glass balls that made your nose look big if you looked into them and we started telling fortunes and all the fortunes were about having big noses and blue faces and then we ate and it was still snowing and the fire and our considerable hot air probably had warmed the windows and when you wiped your hands across them the glass smeared and your hands came away wet. What we were looking for through the window was not the snow it was Father and the wagon. But pretty soon it was just snow and dark outside then more snow and darker and wind and Ginny said all the roads were blocked so we knew we weren't going home a condition with which you might imagine two not-so-tiny boys might be satisfied and we were satisfied. But two days went by and still Father couldn't come and then it was getting on toward late afternoon on Christmas Eve and we were no longer satisfied and neither were our keepers and Johnson had already gotten his ears boxed for displaying some of his dissatisfaction and as a matter of fact when the knock finally came Johnson was standing with his seven-year-old nose in the corner. You can believe me he was the first of us dressed and outside. Now here is where the story really starts. Father was smiling. I had never seen him smile like he was smiling just then. He was standing in the snow next to the horses and I thought his teeth were fixing to fly right out of his head. He had a big lumber sled he'd borrowed from old Cousin Eddie and he and Mother had fixed up a box with colored blankets into which he lifted each of us although neither of us was particularly interested in being lifted and then he said Merry Christmas and thank you and we said Merry Christmas and good-bye and then he covered the box and it was dark though you could see snow through two chinks near the top. Then we could feel that he had turned the team and we were sliding away. I don't suppose he'd done much more than top the first rise when we heard him say woah! and the sleigh stopped and he said ha! and pulled the cover off the box and looked down at us grinning. Then he pulled the present out of his coat and handed it down inside. Open it, he said. We didn't open it straight away. It was wrapped in green foil and had a red ribbon tied around it. We did not have to touch it (or at least I did not have to touch it) to know it was a book. What book is it, Daddy? I said and he said to open it which neither of us showed signs of doing immediately enough so he pulled the present back up and tore off the foil and the ribbon and tossed it away into the snow then handed the book back to both of us and said read what's on the spine. I looked at it. Already it was almost dark. My father leaned forward and lit the lantern. The book was black with gold lettering. I had never seen letters like that. Virgil, I said. I looked up at him. It does not say that, Johnson said. But it did and I asked Father if the book was ours and he said didn't we just unwrap it. Only we had to wrap it back up before Christmas morning because it was supposed to be a surprise. Then he said, open it and read a few lines. I did so. Or started to but couldn't and he said grinning I will teach you that I will teach both of you. I'm cold, Johnson said. That's right, my father said and lifting the book away from me covered the box back up said something to the horses and we began to slide. We slid through the dark in the box and my brother was talking and then he was asleep and then I could hear my father's voice. It was my father's voice reading as he drove and it was sounds I didn't know although I knew it was about my name, Virgil, and then I was asleep and then we had stopped. Father uncovered the box. He was still holding onto the book and told me to stand up and look. We were about three miles from home and it was dark only the sky had cleared and there were stars and a little slice of moon was out and there were about five sleighs with bells and swinging lanterns moving toward us along the road. Then they had said hello and Merry Christmas and we had said hello and Merry Christmas and Johnson had woken up and said what? and Father had lifted him up to see and I was still thinking about those sleighs and lanterns and the pale faces like fire in the colored hoods then we were moving again Father was reading only it sounded now like he was singing Christmas songs like they had been in the sleighs and I was asleep again and then we were home and Mother was shaking us awake and scolding Father for having taken so long and Father grinning and telling us all that it was the happiest Christmas ever and Mother smiling and asking him just what on earth he was up to and taking us each by the coat sleeve and telling us that inside there was cocoa and dinner and hot baths and a decorated tree.

NOAH KEEPS THREE COLOR SLIDES taped to the east window in his bedroom on the second floor of the house in which he was born and in which, with the exception of forty-two days sixty-three years ago, he has lived his entire life. On sunny days, when the light hits them, Noah likes to stand near the window and watch the cubes of color glow then fade like tiny lanterns. Most of the time, however, the slides are black with just the barest hint of color visible. Noah has prepared a slide of himself in which he is standing against a brown and green background looking just off to the left of the camera with his hands in his pockets on a bright blue day last October. He was happy that day. He remembers it quite clearly. Max came over with the camera then fried a couple of hamburger patties for lunch they sat on the back porch Max spotted the cardinal in the crab apple tree they drank a little sweet wine then got in Max's car and drove to the rest home to see Opal. There Max, with Opal smiling throughout the process, made the first mask. Last week, as Noah lay on his back on Ruby's old daybed in the front room, he made the mold for the second.

I want mine decorated, Noah had said.

Decorated how?

Noah thought about it for a while then said, come on. Together, they scoured the house and shed for old coins, bits of colored paper, pressed flowers, the innards of an old, broken watch, dried ladybugs, and wasp wings.

There ought to be something representational about electricity on it, Noah said.

How's that? said Max.

For Opal. I'd stick a damn ice cube on it if I could.

That never happened. They never put her in any ice baths. I've read her file and talked to the doctors.

They say it never happened, said Noah. Don't believe everything you read that's been written by doctors.

They did follow more than one course of electroshock therapy, that's in the file. Apparently they considered but rejected coma-insulin.

You hear what I said about not believing everything doctors write or tell you?

It's true there's no doubt she was better off once you got her out of there.

Should of done it years earlier. Should have been done from the start.

I don't know if a rest place could have served for those earlier years. She was pretty sick.

Noah didn't say anything, shook his head.

A moment later, he looked up.

You probably think this is all foolishness from start to finish.

What's making you say that?

You probably think this is just confirmation of what they all said anyway: that there's some nails missing from my house. Making up masks to bury in drawers and carrying on.

I don't happen to think that, said Max.

Well, why not? said Noah. It's true. Didn't I always try to tell them I was crazy as a jay-lark?

Max started to answer, then didn't say anything.

You must be crazy as a jay-lark to be helping me, said Noah, tapping his finger on the table.

Max raised an eyebrow. Probably, he said.

Noah chuckled. I'll tell you one thing. I don't care how foolish it is. It was her idea and that's good enough for me.

For me too, said Max, smiling. What'd you have in mind about electricity?

Electricity, said Noah. The same as what they kill criminals with. Put diapers on them and such. Ought to lock them damn doctors up. Ought to acquaint them with some of that electricity.

Well, said Max.

Well ain't at all what I had in mind, said Noah.

They festooned the mask with bits of wire and glass from a crushed purple insulator and a tiny diagram from an old pamphlet on making radios with oatmeal boxes. Noah wasn't finished with what he called his "Opal imagery," so they snapped the blade off a paring knife, called it "the scalpel," dipped it in red paint, and glued it on. Noah then had the idea that he wanted, in addition to what she had suffered, to attest somehow to Opal's beauty, so they pulled a peacock feather off of one of Ruby's hats and affixed it to the brow. Then they picked their way through Ruby's costume jewelry and stuck on every bright bit they could find. In one of her letters, Opal had written Noah about Kublai Khan and Xanadu and about the rare flowers she believed must have grown there, so they picked petals off one of the dried bouquets hanging in the attic and, though there wasn't anything particularly rare about them, touched them with glue, found places for them, then stepped back and looked at what they had.

That's looking fine, said Max.

Yes sir it is, said Noah.

You want to do something with hers?

Noah thought a while. He thought about the first time he had seen Opal. Standing on the other side of the dance floor at Gerald and Minnie Roberts's, the light coming down across her, her hands held, slightly open, at her sides. There was heavy mist across what he saw, and he couldn't tell if the mist accentuated or obscured, but either way, he decided, what he saw was cool and clear and clean.

No, he said. Let's leave hers be. I'll have the carnival on mine.

Max said he'd take the mask and treat it so what they'd put on would stay.

Don't go too far with that, I'm going to want it soon.

How do you mean you'll want it soon?

Never mind.

I'll bring it back.

When?

It'll take a few days to get what I need. Early next week.

All right.

That's a fine piece of work, said Max.

It'll do, says Noah.

He picks up the mask and lifts it close enough that his nose and the mask's touch and he can see the stove-lit darkness burning through its eyes.

Dear Noah,

The light lies across us all. It slants and covers us all and we stand together in a field. We all stand and wait. No one comes for us but the light. The electricity does not come for us and we stand and the ice and cold water does not come for us and the light comes across the field and burns us a little but is cool. It is cool like a spoon or a fork when you touch it in the evening. Touch a spoon, Noah. All around us it is snowing but it is warm where we stand and we sing and pretty boys and girls sing and we hold rakes and shovels and it is pretty and nothing but the light comes for us now.

Love, Opal

THE SHERIFF USED TO COME FOR NOAH. Always at night because that was when Noah, who was still seeing things regularly then, saw most clearly, when what he saw might actually, went the theory, be of some use. This too was Virgil's arrangement, an arrangement endorsed by Ruby, who agreed that Noah desperately needed something to take his mind off recent events. At first, Noah and Sheriff Dunn would just sit in the driveway in the near-wreck of a vehicle that served as the county cruiser and the Sheriff would talk and Noah would make the sounds and gestures that meant it was possible he was listening, although mostly, at first, he was not. At first, as the Sheriff talked about missing cars and tools and disputes about who had smacked whom down at the tavern, Noah thought about his walk up to Logansport and about his hands and about Opal, the time they had let him see her, sitting cross-legged and rocking back and forth on her bed in the big ward. Every now and again, though, the Sheriff would say something that Noah would listen to and about every second or third time he would see something and speak. When, for example, the Sheriff brought up the subject of a man under suspicion for having done away with his neighbor's litter of purebred collie pups, Noah saw something he didn't like, something dark and wet and ruined and cold, and he spoke.

He dumped them pups in the creek.

Which creek?

Sugar. Back of his property. Bag's still tied up there. What's left of them pups is still there. Tied to a willow root.

The bag with the drowned pups was found and the neighbor, who had not been able to, he claimed, tolerate their damned "yapping, yapping, yapping," was fined, and the Sheriff came back and talked some more. A week passed. Noah saw something else and reported on it. An arrest was made. They took to driving instead of just sitting in the car.

I reckon I could deputize you, the Sheriff said to Noah one night as they drove the dark county roads. Make your capacity more official.

Would there be any advantage to it besides that?

No.

Then no. I reckon I don't need to be any kind of official.

Well, you know there isn't any other way to see you get some kind of compensation.

Noah didn't say anything.

The Sheriff told him about a botched robbery that had resulted in a woman getting shot.

She dead?

The Sheriff nodded.

Children?

Two of them. Husband's a wreck. He works up at the elevator.

Noah sat there looking at his hands.

Anything? the Sheriff said.

Noah looked over at him.

I want her out.

Now, Noah, you know there's not a damn thing I can do about it. Logansport's not even in my jurisdiction.

You get her out and I'll tell you what I seen.

The Sheriff turned the car around and pretty soon they were back in Noah's driveway.

Is this what this has been about, Noah? Is this why you been riding around with me? I told you when we started I was sorry and that there wasn't anything I could do about it.

You're the law, aren't you?

The Sheriff sighed. I'm the wrong kind of law, Noah. You need a different kind altogether.

They sat there.

After a while, Noah shrugged.

It was the husband shot the wife. It wasn't no botched robbery. He came close to shooting the little girls too. I reckon you'll find some evidence in the kitchen under one or another of the floorboards.

The next night Sheriff Dunn pulled up in the driveway and after a few minutes Noah came out.

Says he got the rifle at an estate auction south of Lebanon. Noah nodded.

The Sheriff asked him if he was going to get in. I reckon not, said Noah.

There's some real good you could do.

You get her out and I'll do all the good you want me to.

That's kind of a mean position, Noah. You sure about it?

Noah looked at the Sheriff then nodded.

Virgil and Ruby in?

Up at church. Singing program. Well, you give them my regards.

It won't do any good to talk to them.

No, said the Sheriff, pulling away, I reckon it won't.

He had tried anyway. Virgil had broached the subject as they were cutting horseweed in the west field. He had not broached it again.

A few weeks later, Noah, whose conscience had started in on him, called the Sheriff and told him that if there were any more murders or such, he was willing to help if he could, and the Sheriff thanked him, but years and years had passed and there hadn't been.

NOAH LIFTS A FINGER and runs it across the glass. He does this twice. Then again, the third time using his nail. For a second, he wishes some part of himself was fast enough to run outside and stare into his own eyes through the glass, then realizes he is already looking at himself, or at least a pale reflection thereof, and that what he sees is even less appealing to countenance than the mask. There was a time, at least to hear Ruby and Opal talk, that Noah went pretty easy on the eyes, especially, apparently, his thick black hair and fine shoulders and strong chin, but that time, if it ever was (and looking into his own near imperceptible reflection he entertains more than a modicum of doubt about this), is long past. The wind has risen and now there is even less to see outside than before. Virgil once stopped late one night like this in the middle of the yard and asked Noah, walking ten or fifteen steps ahead, to turn around and tell him what he saw.

You, said Noah, who was not, at that moment, at all interested. But by the time he reached the house and turned back again, Virgil, who had not moved, was gone and there was only his voice calling,

Can you see me now?

No, says Noah. His hands itch. Where the fingers are gone. Sometimes, though much less frequently than before, the missing digits are still there, he can feel them, as if his hands, he has thought, were slightly haunted—just a bit.

Go away now fingers, Noah says.
    The itching stops.
    Then starts again.

Noah recently saw an advertisement for diamonds that showed a woman's bare hand held against a man's chest, and, printed in big block letters under it,

GIVE HER A DIAMOND, THE HAND LEADS
STRAIGHT TO THE HEART.

Noah remembers holding Ruby's and Virgil's hands, swinging between the two of them on the way to church, or across the driveway, or up the front walk to the house, and he remembers touching each of them on the forehead before their velvet-lined coffins were closed. He remembers, also, touching Opal, and now, holding the double ruin of his hands against the window glass, he cannot help thinking that the messages they have brought back to his heart have long been imperfect. Or perhaps they have been perfect. Perhaps exactly perfect. He cannot tell them apart.

The two tin-roof hog sheds where Virgil kept pigs have long housed only giant spools of green wire, pulled from a small vineyard Noah once kept. Whenever Noah needs some wire he walks out to one of the sheds and clips off a piece. In the summertime, the insides of the sheds are warm and close and smell of old wood and rusted metal. Sometimes, as Noah stands leaning against one of the spools, he closes his eyes and inhales deeply, and just for that moment believes Opal is about to walk up behind him and touch his arm.

Let's go on home now, Noah, she says.

All right, says Noah.

And they walk off through the warm afternoon, hand in hand or arm in arm.

Right now, standing by the window, staring out through the reflection of his own pale eyes into the snowy dark, Noah smells nothing. And when he inhales, the air that enters his mouth and lungs feels distant, strange. Much like the air, Noah thinks, the man in the story must have breathed when, having traveled so far and for so many years simply to reach the bleak ends of the earth, upon instruction from the gods, he killed the black ram.

And then they come, see?
    Yes.
    When he calls them up they come. They have to.
    Why?
    Because of the ram's blood. It is an ancient covenant.
    But he can't touch them.
    That's true. But he can hear them. And he can see.

The windowsill in front of Noah is littered with flies, and the corners of the window are clouded with frozen webs in which Noah can see, faintly glinting in the light from the stove, the tiny, wrapped husks of aphids and fruit flies. In one of the webs a dried, frozen spider lies alongside its prey. Noah reaches up with his left index finger and touches it. Or thinks he does. Either the dead spider is too light or his finger is too cold to tell. One of the many books Virgil read to him as a child was called *Dreams for a Dark Winter,* and in one of the stories, the boy dreaming is dreaming about a wolf, and the wolf in turn is dreaming about him. In the boy's dream the wolf is doing the hunting and eating and in the wolf's it is the boy. Near the end of the story a character called Vulture, acting as go-between, has convinced the two that since each keeps dreaming about the other they must be destined to be friends. But they do not become friends. And at the end of the story Vulture flies away wearing a dark grin.

What we do is not always right.
    Why not?
    I don't know.
    Why can't it always be right?
    Virgil didn't answer.
    Was what you did to us right?
    Yes, I think so. Or I thought so. No. I don't know.

Holding the blunted tip of his finger against the in-folded legs of the spider, Noah can remember lying with his face against the freshly cultivated earth in the middle of a soybean field: It is August and dark and he can hear the others moving through the waist-high soybeans looking for him. They call out to each other. And to him. We'll get you, Noah, they say. He expects them to. Desperately wants them to. Then begins to fear he will vanish into the earth before they can reach him.

Which is what happened to the old gods, said Virgil. After they had been forgotten for a long time they just dropped whatever they were holding, lay facedown on the ground, got still, and after a time the earth opened up and they slipped inside.
    When was that?
    A good while ago.
    What are they doing inside?
    I don't know. Maybe they're dead now.
    Can gods die?
    I think maybe anything can die.

Can you die?

I will die.

Can I?

Noah inhales. The air tastes unbearably rich. A slow, warm wind is moving through the beans, and there are insects all around him. They light on his arms and face and legs. Now, thinks Noah. He lies without moving and can hear the blood beating in his ears.

IN THE SOUTHEAST CORNER OF THE ROOM, next to a cracked, chalk-smeared blackboard, the remains of Ruby's old oven, and a pile of pressure cooker lids, stands a narrow staircase, practically a ladder, that leads up through a hole in the ceiling into a tiny, windowless room. Noah constructed the staircase, cut the hole in the ceiling, and set up drywall to make the room not long after the shed had been built, as a place to keep his special memorabilia. Much like the large room below it, however, its available space was quickly filled, and the mess covering the walls became so general that it is now difficult even for Noah to make sense of it all. In the larger area down below, Noah isn't bothered by the mess, but up here in the tiny room he finds the clutter a little overwhelming. Noah stands with his teeth clenched beneath the single bare bulb and surveys the paraphernalia that surrounds him, trying to get his eye on a photograph he is sure he once tacked up. The photograph, of a small boy dressed in chaps, cowboy hat, and holsters, appeared in the mailbox many years ago. Noah kept it in part because he liked the large, toothless grin the boy wore, but mainly because it came from Opal, who often sent him photographs and ticket stubs and entertainment programs, not to mention packets of paper flowers, occasionally without any letter attached. Sitting by the fire, softened up a little by what he'd been thinking about, Noah had gotten the idea that it would be nice to have the photograph—of Max when he was four or five—in the pocket of his coveralls, so he kicked the pressure cooker lids and an oversize spatula out of the way and climbed the stairs. It bothers Noah that the photograph is not where he thought it would be—between a framed diagram of the solar system and a trio of wildflower seed packets, where instead there is a scrap of paper torn from Virgil's *King Lear,* which reads

Howl! Howl! Howl! Howl! It bothers him, too, that the floor, which is covered with junk and dust, is also littered with dead moths, so many of them that he can't step without crushing one or more. It seems unfair to Noah that the little silver and brown forms, with their curled legs and bent antennae and shredded wings, probably tricked up here sometime when he forgot to turn the light off, should now have to be smashed by him, and he finds himself both wanting to leave immediately and not wanting to move. While he is deciding what to do, he looks over at the north wall, which is where, along with other things, he has tacked up his favorite letters from Opal. Dear Noah, he reads, moving his eye from Dear Noah to Dear Noah to a crudely rendered drawing of a cross section of the human brain to Dear Noah to a photograph of Opal that is too blurred to make out to Dear Noah to Dear Noah to Dear Noah. Also attached to the wall, with a two-inch nail, is the packet of letters he sent to Opal over the years, all but the more recent of which were returned to him by the hospital—which nevertheless allowed Opal to send him letters—unopened. The last he collected along with Opal's other effects when he and Max went up to the rest home. The letters were in a purple box with dried flowers pasted to the outside, which now sits beside Noah's bed in the house.

Noah looks down at his feet, decides where he can place them without causing too much damage, then turns. Or starts to. Because as he is turning he loses his balance, sways, feels his knees go, pitches forward, and ends up on the floor in a heap.

Well, now that didn't help anything, moths or otherwise, Noah says.

He gives a little laugh, embarrassed, then gives another, louder, because he liked the sound of the first.

You should of chewed all this bric-a-brac up, Noah says to the dead moths, a few of which, until he sucks in his breath and blows their dead attention elsewhere, appear, too much like Virgil earlier, to be staring at him. You should of just chewed and chewed and chewed.

Chewed what? Noah asks himself.

All this bric-a-brac, I already said that.

I didn't hear you.

You got ears?

Was that a question or just one of your comments?

Noah doesn't answer. Instead he heaves himself up off his side, brushes dust and dead moths off his pant legs, and starts to stand.

I ain't engaging, he says. Not tonight. That's fine, he answers.

In fact, that might be about all I got to say to you ever.

I've heard that song before.

You think you have, have you? Oh, I have.

Well, never mind. I got a picture to find then I am descending and won't be conversing and carrying on and such.

That picture burned.

No it did not.

Fine, show me where it is.

You got nothing to do with it.

How do you figure that?

Noah isn't sure what to answer. Often, when he holds conversations with himself, he backs himself into a place where it seems difficult to respond. Before he started talking to himself out loud, when the discussions stayed in his mind, Noah would lose argument after argument with himself because he couldn't answer his own questions, or answer quickly enough. He is happy that tonight the exchange didn't end with him launching a tirade of insults at himself, as has often been the case when he comes up short, because he doesn't think he could stand it.

We're done, right? he says.

There is no answer.

Good, he says. Now I just got to find me that picture.

And he does, a moment later. It is lying facedown on the floor with a pair of pliers sitting on it. It is, indeed, partially burned, but not so much that it is disfigured, and Noah stands there a moment staring down into Max's tiny long-ago face.

I'm sorry I contradicted you about it being burned, Noah says.

That's all right, Noah says.

Incidentally . . .

What's that now? I thought we were done.

You know you could just . . .

No.

You sure? It's all set up. You could just grab hold of that hook yonder.

Not like that.

It would allow you to sidestep a fair amount of unpleasantness and foolish miscellany in the hours to come.

I still got things to think about.

Think about! Have you ever in your foolish days done anything else? You reckon you still got things to think about?

I got a plan.

A plan! Is that what you call dozing and talking to the cobwebs?

I said I'm not engaging. Suit yourself.

I aim to.

Noah shrugs, shakes his head, then slips the photograph into the breast pocket of his coveralls and goes back downstairs.

Dear Noah,

I grow wings. Beautiful wings. All different colors. Only instead of growing out and down they grow out and up. Like they're caught at the top. Beautiful, but not right. I'm in a city and I walk down the street and every one of my friends says, when are you leaving? and I say just about as soon as I get these things figured out. I keep walking but the wings are heavy, and I get tired. I lean my forehead against the base of a tall building and, just like in a miracle, I start to rise. Only it's not like I thought. One side of me goes up. Then the other. I look up and I see the wings. The wings are climbing, Noah. The bricks move past my face. They are bright red. Then all of a sudden my head hits against a cornice and everything goes black. And after a minute I can see myself. I'm just hanging there and those wings are climbing. It must be one of those big buildings. They just keep moving up and up.

Love, Opal

NOAH LOOKS OVER HIS SHOULDER, shivers a little, then sits. The chair creaks as he settles, then is quiet. Noah takes one or two deep breaths and clears his throat. The stove door is now closed, and Noah can see pieces of flame moving behind it. It looks to him, when he sees them moving slowly or quickly, or sometimes both at the same time, like the fire, which this late at night must be fast asleep, is dreaming. Above the grate, stamped into the black metal, is a row of soot-filled stars. Max's Egyptian cat has been joined by several others. One of them, a lean calico, has brought in half a mouse and from time to time hits at it with her paw. All the cats look at Noah. Noah looks around the room. It makes the corner of a large implement shed that sits on the foundations of a barn built by Noah's great-grandfather, a farmer and circuit rider who died of a heart attack just before stepping into the pulpit a few years after the Civil War. The barn had been among the largest in the county and Noah had loved its sagging boards and dark corners and deep smells. When, shortly after Ruby's death, it burned, due, according to the official report, to faulty wiring, three fire trucks emptied their tanks into the blaze before they got it stopped. The new shed was built on part of the old foundation using the lower half of what was left of one wall. Halfway up the older part of the wall, visible from Noah's seat in front of the stove, "Noah and Opal Summers, 1937" is painted in Opal's neat black letters, though the "1937" is now hidden behind part of a chair. The room is crowded with piles and boxes and the tools that escaped the fire and the burned or partially burned remains of some that did not. Almost as soon as the new shed was built Noah began filling it. At one point, just like with the little room upstairs, he had a system. Now the only system is to try not to overly obstruct the door. Some days, Max comes and digs through the piles of debris. Once, he found an old tape recorder and, sitting in airtight canisters, a few reels of tape. He came back with them a week later, and the two of them listened to a faint recording of Noah and Virgil talking, and of Ruby singing hymns.

I presume that was afterwards.

Noah didn't answer.

After Opal went away.

Noah didn't answer.

Max leaned forward and turned up the volume.

That was some kind of a voice Ruby had.

The recorded conversation between Noah and Virgil was about a book Virgil had been reading called *Raintree County*, which Virgil claimed was "a kind of retelling of the history of the universe as seen through the eyes of a citizen of the republic who for once is by design a Hoosier and who is both brilliant and a fool."

Speak a little louder, Noah's voice said.

It is a fine enough work, Virgil said, now yelling. Though I think the hero is a little too brilliant and not quite enough the fool. It is also a touch on the ponderous side. You might enjoy setting it on the scales.

Will you make me go out to the chicken house if I do?

Tell you what, you tote that heifer up to the scales, and I'll go out to the chicken house and sit with you. Noah liked listening to the laughter this exchange provoked, so much so that when Max asked him why he was chuckling, he discovered he couldn't stop chuckling and, after a moment, had to get up and walk around.

The other day, not long after he discovered the packet of flowers, Max dug up a fuse box that for years had hung at the back of the broom closet in the house. The small golden-brown box was almost as deep as it was wide, and painted in bright red at the top center of the lid was a circle and inside the circle were the words "Arrow Hart." Max removed a screw and the lid came off easily. Behind it was a square of wires and empty fuse-sockets, and Max looked at this for a moment then spoke the two words aloud, "Arrow" then "Hart," making Noah, who could not take his eyes off the now useless contents, think of a television program he had seen that proposed, although no one could yet say why, that the universe was expanding, that it would expand then contract, faint red then faint blue, in endless repetitions, like a heart grown infinitely huge.

Everywhere in the shed there is the faintly pleasant smell of gasoline mixed with the slightly less pleasant smell of oil.

Repeat, said Virgil.
Noah repeated.
No, said Virgil.
Noah said it again.
No, said Virgil.
Noah told him the floor was still falling.
No, said Virgil.
Noah repeated it.
The floor is not falling.
Say it.
The floor is not falling.
Say it again, quickly.
The floor is not falling. The floor is not falling.

But the floor was falling. It fell faster.
I want her back, God damn you, said Noah.
Hush now, said Virgil.
The floor, rushing, fell.

Dear Opal,

I got your letter with the flowers in it. Thank you. They sure do look interesting. I want to try the flowers but the package is so pretty it would be a shame to tear it. You ask me what I am doing. I have been listening to the radio lately. Also I have been working on tearing out fencerows. I don't like to do it when there are morning glories on the fence, so usually I just leave those stretches. Ruby is fine. She is in at the television and sends her regards. I hope they let me come up and see you again soon. Is your eye still orange? I don't like the sound of that. This morning I went out to where our house was and I saw you standing there pretty as ever. I miss you.

Dear Opal,

That was some whirlwind you wrote about. I think I know what you mean about whirlwinds. I think I got a whirlwind in my head sometimes. Certainly, it is filled with whoosh. I don't have much else to say. I always miss you.

Dear Opal,

Virgil won't talk about it so I'm not going to talk to him. It's been a week now and I have not said a word to him pretty much and I reckon I may never speak to him again. I was helping the Sheriff out but then he wouldn't help me back so I have stopped. Ruby says I ought to pray. I have prayed. But still you are not here and we do not take our walk together in the evening. Your step-daddy said I couldn't come back on his property until I had figured out my manners again. I am afraid it is true that I wasn't necessarily as decent to him as I should have been the last time I went up there to try and get him to sign what has to be signed before they'll let me see you again. Was all that really in bloom like you described it? I went out there and checked and sure enough the tulips we planted were blooming. I been seeing a lot of things lately. I been having some bad spells. I'm not talking to Virgil but he has been helping me out some. He will read this letter over to make sure I got it all down to some extent correctly. I know it isn't right to hate but I reckon maybe I hate him, even though it doesn't sit well. I am sorry that this letter isn't much. I miss you and want you home.

Dear Opal,

I miss you. Today I had a bad spell and acted what Virgil said was inappropriate at my job delivering the mail. Virgil reckons I may have gotten myself fired and is not too content with me. When I was driving I thought about you like usually I do but this time I thought a little harder and that was where I reckon I got pickled up. The daylilies are up and the chicory and they wave in the wind. I ate my dinner with folks I was only supposed to deliver mail to. They had dogs and some sons that got themselves killed off at the war. I knew those boys. Virgil talked to me considerably when I got home. He went back out with me and we got it delivered straight then I went up to my room and looked at your picture and some of the little things you sent me that I keep special. Then I crawled under my bed and laid up there a little with my eyes closed then everything stopped moving and I got out and now I am writing you.

Dear Opal,

I am glad they are letting you have my letters. I hope this new home will be comfortable and that you will be well and happy there and I expect you know I am sorry I didn't get you there sooner. I hope that you will get used to it. I kept all the letters they sent back to me from Logansport and if you like I can send them again. Maybe that's just old memories though. I will keep them then if you do come and visit you can take them if you want to. In the connection with visitors, I had one the other day. This was Steve Shanks I met a long time ago

on that walk I took up to see you. He displayed quite a fair amount of kind-
ness toward my direction on that walk and I was happy to see him again. He
is about as old as a body can get now and having considerable trouble with his
eyes. I had some cherry pie left over that Candy Wilson had brought me over
and I gave him some of that. There wasn't really much to it only he was still
carrying on despite his years and his hard spells and we had a fine time. I had
seen something about him that time and it had come to pass and I was very
sorry to hear that it had. But generally he was in fine shakes and we had quite
a time. I hope you will come and visit me. Let me know what they say when you
ask them. I expect we could have quite a time too.

Dear Opal,

I think it is a fine idea and not silly at all. I had about forgotten about that gal
with her elixirs and notions and masks and what you wrote me about that fellow
coming out of the corn without any face on jimmied it back in my head. I will
put them here together in a special place. They can just stay here in the shed and
commemorate us and we'll go on about our business wherever it is we're going.
Max says he'll take the cast for yours when we come up to see you a week from
Tuesday. He says he studied up on it in a book and that there isn't necessarily
much trick to it. I will put mine on then take it off and set it next to yours just
like you dreamed. I miss you fierce. I'm glad I can come and see you now.

Dear Opal,

You are right that these letters are taking me a long time to set down. Virgil
offered to write what it is I have to say but I figured it would be about as well if
I kept at it with him smoothing over my scrawl. Ruby said it just takes motiva-
tion like anything else and now with you away for a while I got it. I been having
my troubles with you gone and I been resting up and having trouble with falling

over and seeing things like usual only it's about all the time now. Quite a bit of the time just lately it is the floor falling out from me and it seems like I'm just falling down with it to hell. I had a couple incidents out in the fields to do with my hands. Did I ever tell you what that old fellow up at Hillisburg said about the Finger Lady? Well, like he said, it was just a story and didn't change a thing. I am waiting for you to come home and I will feel fine again. I will build us a new place better than the old one. I have already told Ruby this and she told Virgil because I am not speaking to him most days, and they both agreed though they said I should wait to get started until you get here. We'll set out pretty things all around the house. I got some seed catalogues we can look through. There will be big windows and a spot for us both to sit together in the light.

NOAH LOOKS AROUND at the piles on the floor and at the cats on the workbench and at the tools hanging from the walls. He walks over to the wall, eyes the big saw, pulls it off the hook, runs his thumb across the teeth. Then taps his nail on the flat of the blade making it ring. Noah knew a saw player once. Saturday mornings as a boy Noah would ride into town with Virgil to sell vegetables. They would set up their table on a strip of grass between the tracks and the road across from the half block of tired-out red-brick buildings that made up downtown. It was never very long before Virgil set off in search of a "little friendly discourse," leaving Noah to count pennies and nickels and, from time to time, hand over fat tomatoes and boxes of green beans and heavy ears of sweet corn. One slow morning after Virgil had left, Noah looked up over a pile of muskmelons and saw a wrinkle-faced fellow sitting on a low stool across the deserted street grinning at him.

You ever hear someone play a saw? the man said.

Noah looked at him. He didn't say anything. Then shook his head.

No, I bet you ain't, the man said. He grinned. There was a purple case with a bright red saw painted on it leaning against the wall beside him.

Ain't like nothing you ever heard, said the man. That's a fact.

What's it like? said Noah.

The man looked at his fingernails, then up at Noah. You want to hear?

Noah nodded.

Tell you what—you fetch me over one of them melons you got there and I'll play you a tune.

Melons are a nickel, said Noah.

A tune's a nickel, so if you fetch me over exactly one of them melons we're square.

Noah looked at the purple case then at the man then back at the case.

Is it in there? said Noah.

The man leaned over, unfastened the lid of the case, and pulled it open. Then he took out the saw and pulled a stick with a yellow knob attached to it out of his pocket.

Noah picked up one of the melons.

Ah, said the man, that looks like a good one, and before Noah had cleared the table, he had started to play, the stick gliding up and down the curved saw, filling the air Noah walked through holding the heavy, sun-warmed melon with the strangest sounds.

Noah set the melon down in front of him and the saw player grinned and continued to play and Noah felt like he had walked into the middle of a pool of warm metal and that half of the pool was square and the other half round.

You like that, son? the saw player asked after he had stopped moving the stick and had set the saw across his lap.

Noah nodded. Then that's fine.

The saw player wore faded coveralls and had thin wrists and big feet and only four fingers on his right hand.

On the ground beside him sat a jug.

What's in there? Noah asked.

That's just tractor oil mixed with lung liniment. I need it for playing.

Where's your finger?

You mean this one? said the saw player, raising his right hand and wiggling the stump of the missing finger around. You mean this one that ain't there?

Noah nodded.

That's quite a story, said the saw player. I reckon we'll save that.

Can I look at your saw?

The saw player looked down at the saw and raised an eyebrow.

What else you got over there?

I got some cucumbers.

No. Uh, uh. Don't like cucumbers.

How about radishes? We pulled them up this morning.

Radishes? You want a look at this fine instrument for some radishes! We're talking business here, son. A trade's a trade. Now, are those some fine-looking tomatoes I see?

Noah ran back across the street, picked out two of the biggest tomatoes, and brought them over.

All right, said the saw player. That's fine and them's handsome tomatoes and I do appreciate it and I can see that you've got the makings in you of a businessman. Now, come on over close, let's take a look at this here saw.

The instrument Noah was allowed to hold for approximately thirty seconds was a three-foot large-tooth saw that the saw player claimed his grandfather had used trimming sequoias in California before the Civil War. Noah tried to picture sequoias. The following Saturday the saw player brought a page torn from an illustrated magazine. Men and women in picnic clothing standing in the middle of a forest of giant trunks. Noah asked if the forest was real and the saw player said, Didn't I just say it was, and Noah asked if he could show the picture to his father. Virgil said there was such a forest, though he would not say whether or not he thought it was true that the saw had once been used on such trees—he said he had one or two reservations on that. The saw was beautiful, everyone who passed by commented on it. The saw player had painted the handle with stars and moons and he had cleaned and polished the blade. When he played, the steel shone. He played. The strange sound came out of the shining steel and people began to walk even more slowly than they had been. By and by a small crowd gathered. The street slowed down. Noah, sitting behind his vegetables, thought of sequoias. And of the men and women in picnic clothing. It was a warm, sunny morning in distant California but deep at the bottom of the sequoias it was cool and dark. Anyone could say anything and the sound would come away soft. They spoke. The men to the women. The women to the men. Off in the far distance there was the small sound of men at work with saws. The earth below the men and women's feet was cool and smooth and gave as they moved across it. Someone had brought a gramophone. The black disk spun and the music came out into the cool, strange light. The people danced. Colors played across them. As if the air had divided itself, taking all it contained with it. Oxygen and nitrogen here. Carbon and helium there. Slow then fast. Fast then slow. The people danced then fell. All of them, eventually, fell.

IN ONE OF THE STORIES Virgil told Noah during that period, a group of soldiers had been tracking a group of Indians. These Indians had committed some crime or had been accused of committing some crime or might at some point come to be accused. The soldiers, in tracking the Indians, had ridden across the northern hills and prairies, and they had crossed and recrossed rivers, sometimes in a steamboat.

What was the boat's name?
The *Far West.*

They had ridden and crossed and held camp under the stars and woke and made coffee under a different dark sky the stars now changed and ridden again and camped again and sung in low voices and smoked and spoke of far-off foyers and meals and quiet fires and silver lamps and dresses of silk and gingham and all around them that dark not-at-all-imagined immensity and again above them those stars. Then they had the trail. Alleluia, boys, said the commanding officer. The trail ahead of them looked, some of the soldiers said afterwards, like a herd of angry giants had passed, but the commanding officer, whose boots and spurs were afterwards sold to a museum, pressed on.

In another story there was a war raging in the South and at a crucial moment during this war one of the commanders screamed and threw himself from a high window onto a rocky slope leaving behind instructions to his lieutenants that the key to victory would be revealed by the positioning of his broken limbs. The opposing army was just cresting a nearby ridge. A woman, the favorite slave of the dead commander, was called forth. The woman's hands moved through the air in front of her face a few times as if to clear it then she looked down. When she saw what lay with its head crushed and limbs splayed she wailed once, lifted her skirts, and leapt down. All afternoon the battle raged around and over them. At the end of it, though no one could say why, the dead commander's forces had won. When Virgil finished this story he said something in Latin and Noah asked him what he had said (The End) then asked him how many languages there were (more than you would care to count). They went outside. It was a clear night, and Virgil explained to Noah that what they saw was light, and that light should never be mistaken for its progenitor, stars. Those, he said, we never see. He then said, despite this inherent disjunction we are simultaneously made of and made possible by those stars and by our star specifically, the Sun.

What? said Noah.

They stood there. It was summer and hot and the cicadas were screaming in the hickories. So much noise down here, Virgil had said, another time, another night.

They stood there. This night. Virgil not answering, or, possibly, it occurred much later to Noah, offering as answer the incomprehensible arrangements above his head.

I can see you want to ask me something, said Virgil. Go on ahead and ask. I don't promise any answer.

Why did the commander jump?

Because the woman had to jump. It was an arrangement. Like an orchestration. A piece of tragic choreography. A mostly forgotten symphony of love and war.

You need music for a symphony.

No, you don't.

Yes, you do.

Well, if you do, and I'm not in agreement on that, they had cannon and gun flash and screams.

I don't understand, said Noah.

Virgil said nothing.

I don't understand any of it, said Noah.

You won't, said Virgil finally. Neither will I.

After appearing three Saturdays in a row, the saw player told Noah he reckoned he'd had his run and would be moving on.

Moving on where? said Noah.

The saw player took a swig of his tractor oil and shrugged. You got any suggestions?

California, said Noah.

California, said the saw player, now there you got you a thought.

You didn't tell me about your finger yet.

Didn't I? said the saw player.

Noah shook his head.

The saw player took another drink then asked Noah what he'd heard about the Finger Lady and whether or not he had an opinion on her.

The what? said Noah.

Now don't you go on and tell me you never heard about the Finger Lady.

I never did, said Noah.

Well, now, that's a shame, that is indeed, and I reckon we'd better rectify it directly. You bring me on over one of your daddy's fine tomatoes and I'll see if I can't tell you the long of it good and short.

Noah brought over a tomato. The saw player lifted it up to his mouth and bit into it like it was an apple.

Then he told Noah about the Finger Lady.

My daddy would like that story, Noah said.

Is that a fact?

He likes stories that don't make regular sense.

Well then I reckon he likes most stories.

Noah thought about this then nodded.

Is that all you asked her for is that saw?

Case too, said the saw player. But if you're going to ask for more than one thing you have to ask for it all in the same breath and you can't ask too much or she won't give you nothing and then you're just out a finger with squat-twiddle to show.

Why'd she take her own fingers off at night in the first place?

Because they were so fine and pretty she was afraid they'd get mussed if she slept on them.

What was the sister's name?

What sister?

That put glass and pepper in them while she was asleep so she couldn't ever put them back on?

I didn't say it was her sister, I said it was her neighbor. You always ask this many questions?

Noah nodded then said, It's better if it's her sister.

So why'd she do it? the saw player asked.

I don't know, said Noah. I never heard the story before.

The saw player laughed then leaned forward. Twyla, I reckon the jealous sister's name was Twyla, he said.

My mother had a friend named Twyla.

Did she?

She did until she got too sick and moved away. Are you leaving now?

The saw player had stood up and put his case under his arm.

Time to go, he said.

What about your whiskey?

Tractor oil and lung liniment is what it was. And anyway, it's all done. I reckon I'll get some more fuel when I get out to California.

You ain't going to California.

Who says I ain't?

Noah shrugged. You're going over to Colfax, he said. You're going to set next to the bank and say something and the sheriff's going to roust you.

The saw player laughed. You just remember, you get yourself in a fix, or there's something you just got to have, you offer you up something sweet to the Finger Lady and she'll come flying down and do you right.

You want another tomato? said Noah.

I do, said the saw player. But I'll ask a different favor first.

What? said Noah.

I want you to promise me you won't believe a word I just said.

NOAH TRIED PLAYING the saw that afternoon, though his rusty old saw sounded nothing like the saw player's. This was frustrating, but he kept at it, sitting there with his legs dangling over the edge of the haymow, looking out through the window at the tops of white oaks and small, scattered clouds. He sat there and played and thought about commanders jumping out of windows and smashed clocks and flag-wrapped remains. He thought about seeing things that were both there and not there and he pressed the saw against his fingers as he thought. He pressed the saw lightly then not so lightly against the base of one or two of his fingers and thought about his mother leaning over the huge family Bible like she was fixing to jump into it and he thought about the peoples that had once lived out in the open on these lands and were now gone. He said, Oh Finger Lady, Finger Lady, like the saw player had told it, but couldn't think of anything he wanted or any fix he was in and after a time, before any real damage had been done, laid off. He spent the afternoon in the barn and, when called for supper, came back with the base of his fingers covered in dried blood. Ruby screamed then said a short prayer then told Virgil to get soap and bandages. After they had wrapped his hands, Virgil said, Why did you do it? and Noah said, I don't know, I saw the walls shimmering. Then I was shimmering. As if the air had divided itself.

It suddenly occurs to Noah that he is hungry, that he can't remember when or what he last ate, that the situation should be dealt with as quickly as possible. He would like to eat some corn, or peas, though not the frozen kind that sits in small plastic boxes in the deep freeze. What he wants is an ear of sweet corn, its kernels bursting with moisture and sweetness, or a tomato so ripe it has split in two or three places, or a fistful of raw snow peas with their ends snapped off. A melon would be nice. A juicy muskmelon pulled out of the garden that morning and setting in the refrigerator all day to chill. Or spinach. Huge sweet leaves of spinach tossed into a salad. Noah has the fixings, he must have, somewhere in the kitchen. Even a carrot would do. Not some wilty old thing that's been sitting in the crisper next to some played-out celery and apples for weeks, but an honest to goodness garden-fresh carrot ready to scrub and peel and eat. Noah closes his eyes and can taste carrot. He can feel bits of it under his tongue and pressing against his teeth. He starts to think about fresh-slaughtered meat, dripping off the bone, and stops himself—it's too much. Instead, he holds up an imaginary ear of corn, its kernels shining golden in the stove light, salt and pepper caught in the almost melted butter, then brings it to his mouth and bites. Nothing. Noah lets his hands drop. He sees he is still holding the saw. He runs his thumb along the blade again and looks around.

If one of you cats was to move wrong I'd eat you, he says.

God damn it, I don't rightly know what I'm doing, he says.

After hanging the saw back up and looking around for a while, he finds a half tower of saltines leaning up against an old dead lamp and begins mashing them, one by one, into his mouth.

I DIDN'T MAKE THIS UP—someone told it to me. It's a Fifty-Percenter for sure. Once upon a time, a man saw a black and silver storm flashing darkly off at the horizon. It was still there, darkly flashing, when some hours later he left off his work and looked again. At dinner, he mentioned the storm to his wife, who said, I see, then left the table to stand a moment at the window, before sitting down again and asking if he would care for more okra. I would care for more okra, thought the man. The next morning the storm had moved closer. Each day then it moved closer. Tomorrow, I reckon, the man said. His wife spent much of the morning in her room and then on the telephone, and in the afternoon her brother's truck came and she went away. That night the man sat out late on the porch and watched the lightning, still off at some distance, smash silently, over and over again, into the corn. Watching, he dozed and dreamed that the thunder had gotten held up on another job and couldn't make it this time, but sent its regards. In the morning the storm was gone. Or it wasn't. No it certainly wasn't. As he was pumping water for the pigs, he saw a shredded line of white light slice through one of the elephant oaks in the west woods. Letting go of the pump handle, he began to walk toward it, talking to himself as he walked:

One witness said that what you see at first until your eyes are adjusted is a swarm of triangles and circles and other, various, compositions of light. The light, presumably freed of any impetus to illuminate, layers itself, an accumulation of colors that soon separate, pulling everyone, gently, apart.

Another said it was like looking down into a cyclone. At the middle of it everything was still. And then it was not still. And then: everything.

Another said: I saw a lake of fire, black and bubbling, and souls streaming in an imperfect arc over the flames from one bank to the other.

Another: White. Everything was white. We were all there. All of us.

ON THE AFTERNOON of his eighteenth birthday, after the meal and cake and present—a .22 caliber single-shot rifle—Noah was told, at his request, each of his parents taking part in the telling, that he had been born a breech birth. He had, in fact, been stillborn in what was now the dining room, but had been "woken" by Virgil at the kitchen sink as the doctor worked feverishly at the bed.

No you were *not* born dead, said Ruby.

After his parents told him this, Noah began collecting the wings of all the dead wasps he could find, plucking them up like desiccated jewels from the scatterings of dead flies that covered the windowsills in the attic, the barn, the chicken house. Joining the gently sloped tips with clear-drying China glue he fashioned two small almond-shaped lenses that he had both his parents look through once (When it happens, when I see things, it looks like that, like seeing and not-seeing both, he said) and then crushed.

Not long after this, as they were trying out the new rifle (in the woods and mist, the early light seeming to rise up out of the ground around them), Virgil told him he had read of a group of people long ago who had believed that at the beginning of death directions on how to proceed were given to departing souls.

Is that what's happening to me? Noah asked. Have I been getting directions?
There's nothing like that happening to you.
Then how do you explain it?
I don't.

Don't or can't?

Both.

That evening as he sat at the table cleaning the rifle (which
had performed, Virgil had opined, very satisfactorily), Ruby,
cleaning the squirrels (their bodies contained so little blood
that when Noah dreamed, some time later, that like Odysseus
he was calling forth the dead, and had only a squirrel to
sacrifice, all he could call forth was an arm, a leg, a chin, a
nose), told Noah that there were good clear directions for
Noah to be found in any one of the Bibles they had in the
house.

Go and fetch one, said Virgil.

That won't prove anything, said Ruby.

Go and fetch one, Noah.

Noah did.

Read, said Virgil.

Noah opened the Bible. The words swam.

Ruby said it didn't matter. She said some things took time.
It didn't matter if he couldn't read yet. He'd learn well enough
before long. Anyway, he'd been baptized. In those few drops
of water was all the direction he'd ever need.

IN THE SECOND to last letter Opal sent Noah she described

a whirlwind bathed in bright light in which she could see, fiercely spinning,
earth and rock and corn and tree and house and car and tractor and lantern
and cow and flower and weed and root and vegetable and knife and hoe and
river and plate and fork and crock and closet and book and bones and sink
and rose and dandelion and dog and mantis and spider and fly and church and
rose . . .

I KNOW THAT THE ANCIENT PERSIANS, said the Minister, many, many years after Noah's eighteenth birthday, after Virgil and Ruby were gone, and the Minister was an old, gray cancer-ridden needle of a man in a rocker by a west-facing window holding a bottle of something strong, I know that the ancient Persians, said this Minister to Noah, who had come after years of absence from the church to see him, worshiped the Sun, plain and simple, and that way they knew when they got burned or froze to death they'd done something wrong, though what *wrong* meant to them, I do not know. The Greeks had it figured out that it was all already decided and all you could do, if you were lucky, and only heroes were ever lucky, was hold something off, or believe you were. They didn't do a very good job at first of holding the Persians off, although later, presumably because they were supposed to, they did. And if the wrath of the Persians had been something awesome to behold, what boiled up out of those be-plumed righteous sons of pagan Heaven when their turn came was dark and beautiful both. Them Greeks were something else. They'd go anywhere. First though they would slit the throat of just about anything that moved and then pour wine and water on the ground. That's what you call a sacrifice. I suppose that this was the source of a lot of other throat slitting that has since gone on. Think of the Romans. I don't imagine you are aware of what kind of travails your early ancestor Christians were up against. I did in fact once have a dream in which I was an ancient Christian and the rest of the dream was a fire. God now embraces all of it anyway and that includes pain and that includes everything that isn't pain and all of it praise the Lord is His and is holy. That cross you would see behind me every Sunday if you came to church is as close to a divining stick as you will get on this earth and you will notice that it does not point in any particular direction and that is to say it is pointing all around. Your father knew that. He knew it and he categorically rejected it. Do you know how that man your earthly father spent his free time? Are you aware of what he got up to?

That was when he was younger, said Noah.

The Minister looked at him.

You really think he straightened himself out? You really think he stopped thinking, even if he stopped talking?

Noah didn't answer.

All right, he said. Everyone, I reckon, knew it and, well, it doesn't matter now and, more's the better, never mind. I will say this, though. I think, finally, the Holy Father opened up a big hole in that pig head of his and pulled his brain right out. That's justice. Our Lord knows justice, that he does. In ancient times they went into caves and asked old ladies which way the world was turning and what they ought to do about it and all I can tell you is that no matter how often those old ladies were correct in their counsel every time they opened their godless mouths those old cave ladies and their interpreters lied. I grew up in a church in Kentucky that was all smoke and that was all holy brimstone and my minister used to tell us not to worry, that in the end it was all truth because it had never been anything but truth and that in the center of God's palms (sinners on the left, saints on the right) we'd all be pressed clean and that it would all be reduced (he pressed his palms together), in that reckoning, to a finger-length of fire. His to blow out or affix to his crown.

Here the Minister, coughing, stopped, took a large sip of his drink, coughed some more, then wiped his eyes and looked at Noah.

I understand you have been known to make certain auguries, he said. What can you tell me about my lungs?

I'd like to know about my wife, said Noah.

My lungs, son, are they black? How long do I have?

I came here to ask you about my wife, said Noah. I just now learned they have been giving her electricity and putting her in ice baths.

The Minister turned away from Noah, took another drink, looked back out his window, and said, You know who you should have asked about that.

I did, said Noah.

Well, what'd he say?

He said it couldn't be helped. That someone might of got killed.

Prayer would've helped.

My mother prayed.

She was a good woman, your mother. Hers would have been a powerful prayer. But it was for you to pray, Noah Summers. It was your prayer that would have been attended up in that blessed realm where the angels sit and dream of light. Did you pray?

You were in love with my mother, said Noah.

That's slander, son. Do you know what *slander* means?

Noah didn't answer.

The purest slander.

Noah thanked the Minister then turned to leave.

You should've prayed for Opal's recovery, Noah Summers.

Noah put his hand on the doorknob.

The Minister said, Wait.

Noah took his hand off the doorknob, turned.

I been hard on you, the Minister said. More than I should. I shouldn't have talked about your daddy that way. That wasn't right. Not least because it has apparently put slanderous notions about my interest in your mother's soul and salvation in your head. I know what the Lord has seen fit in his wisdom to gift you with hasn't always been easy. You come to ask me about she who you call your wife, and I will give you your answer as I know it.

All right, said Noah.

The Minister turned his head toward the window and moved his lips then, after a moment, turning back toward Noah and fixing him with eyes that poured out from under his high forehead, said, God is everything and everywhere. She will neither burn nor drown.

Holding his eyes steady with only slight movements to the right and left makes Noah tired. Sometimes, Noah is so tired it feels as if his bones have left his body—have left behind a pile of skin and white hair and worn-out coveralls.

Go look at something else, Noah says to the cats.

Scat, he whispers.

The air around his mouth is cold, so that his teeth hurt slightly, and he can hear the glass shifting in the windows. Noah closes his eyes. The glass shifts. He opens them. He leans forward, closer to the stove, and realizes that the cats are gone.

Whoosh, whispers Noah.

Around him, in the gloom, the walls and piles glisten. Much like they glistened just after Noah wrapped the bad stretch of wire in straw and set a match to it and watched as it began to burn. Strangely, although the fire department came and the Sheriff came and he told them and even yelled it that he was responsible for the fire that it was his fire he was crazy and he had started it and he was plum crazy and Virgil and

Ruby were dead now and they had better send the hospital to come God damn get him at last, the fire department had left and the Sheriff had left and the hospital had not come. Only the neighbors came, some to look at what was left of the barn and some to look at him.

Here, shake my hand, I'm plum damn crazy, it's the circus right here in my head, he said to them, but they did not take his hand. They just muttered and told him to watch himself and shook their heads.

One of them, Zorrie Underwood, who lived the next farm over, came every day for two weeks and brought Noah dinner. She would sit with Noah as he ate and say nothing and just look at him.

I'm crazy, Zorrie, I burned that God damn barn down on purpose, Noah would say.

I would count it a favor if you didn't use ill-colored words, Zorrie would say.

One afternoon, as Noah was coming back from hammering a couple of nails into the old corncrib at the edge of the east woods, he found Zorrie standing under the crab apple tree, her arms crossed over the front of a pretty blue dress, waiting for him.

I don't care if you are crazy, Noah, she said.

Noah didn't say anything.

We're both of us alone, she said.

Your Emerson's dead, Zorrie Underwood, Noah said after a minute. My Opal isn't.

Twice the Sheriff came by.

You better send them, Noah told him, it was always me that was the crazy one. You know I see things most of which aren't there and never were and I swallow my tongue and now I've set a fire too.

The second time the Sheriff came he told Noah that Virgil and Ruby had insured the barn and that the insurance had been kept current and the official report was that faulty wiring had been responsible. He would make the necessary arrangements for a new structure to be erected around the remnants of the old.

Before he left, he put a hand on his hip, tipped back his hat, and said, I hear Zorrie Underwood's been getting you your supper these last days.

Noah said, Yes sir she is, but now she isn't coming anymore.

Isn't coming anymore?

No sir.

Why not?

Because I'm married's why. I got a God damn wife.

Now, there's no cause to shout, Noah.

I want you to take me—call them up and tell them to take me to the hospital. Or I'll go myself, just tell them to expect me. Tell them to let me in. I'll pay you. I got money saved. It's in the house. You can have it.

We been through this, Noah, a long time ago. You can have every last cent.

The Sheriff had looked long and hard at Noah, shook his head, then pushed his hat back down and climbed into his car.

When the new shed was finished, the Sheriff came by a third time and inspected the shed and spat and said, Now Noah I don't care if you are crazy, and you just might be, but you done set your fire and you aren't going to set any more.

This has proved true. Noah hasn't. He isn't entirely sure why, but suspects he had just the one fire in him.

Besides, he likes the shed. He liked it when it was new and empty and the walls still smelled of paint, and he likes it now

when it smells of gasoline and oil and is filled with imple-
ments and objects and the light from the stove. Noah likes
the shed. Noah puts another log on the fire. Noah pulls his
fingers into small, broken fists. Noah moans.

ONCE UPON A TIME THERE WAS A MAN. Once upon a time there was a woman. Once upon a time there was a man and a woman and then there wasn't. That's all I know about that.

Dear Noah,

It is a crown.
(crown crown crown)

A tall crown.
(tall tall tall)

There are bright jewels and dark jewels.
(bright bright bright)

The steel shines like teeth.
(teeth teeth teeth)

The gold shines like fire.
(fire fire fire)

Love, Opal

NOAH SITS DOZING in front of the stove. He dreams. In the dream the tool-covered walls of the inner room grow translucent and, after a moment, Noah can see people there. Behind the people is another wall, and behind that wall more people, endless. All the people move, slowly, from side to side, and they all watch him. Noah's leg jerks and he wakes and when he wakes he is a young man and is standing with other young men and young women in a circle on a shining floor. Then music starts, music that Noah cannot hear, but that must have started, because suddenly they all begin to move. Dear Noah. They all move. Quickly. Noah glides or attempts to glide in and out of the others and then, as if he had entered a story, his arms go around a young woman's waist. *The knight meets the furled lady. He desires her. She desires to elaborate on his lineage so they both advance through the green groves merrily until they meet. They meet.* And then he is walking slowly across a gravel barn lot with the young woman named Opal and then into the deep shadow of a corn bin and then into Opal's arms. *And they all dance a carole that breaks into a farandole they all dance a moonlit carole that breaks into a merry farandole until someone dies unto Dieu then they all through the green groves, sadly, retreat.*

That's pleasant, the young woman says. She is tall, with coal-black hair and coal-blue eyes and fine arched eyebrows that just seem to rise and rise. Her family has just moved down to Tipton from Cass County to take over an ailing relative's farm. She smells good. Like mint and basil and lilac blended. They walk together or stand and speak quietly or do not speak.

Well then, you will have to come and call on me, Noah Summers, she says when the evening has come to its end and everyone is moving to their cars. She says, you come and see me, Mr. Noah Summers. It isn't much to look at, but we have a hundred acres just like you do and we have a horse and on the front porch we have a swing.

Noah took the truck over to Tipton to see the swing. And, once she'd crammed half a piece of warm pecan pie into his mouth, instructing him, as he did so, not to chew if he could help it, and had had him wash it down with a glass of buttermilk, he walked with her across the hundred acres. They stood in the rain together and looked out over a small, windswept bean field together and walked single file together through the corn. The corn blades brushed against their faces.

I like that, the young woman said.

I liked that pie and buttermilk, Noah said.

Everything was perfect. It was a cool evening in late summer. Noah put his hands on her face. He still had his fingers. His fingers ran the ridges of her face and she smiled.

I one hundred percent like it when you do that, she said.

I one hundred percent like that your name is Noah, she said, and I wish we were on a raft or could float like ducks or swans or Canada geese and it would pour.

Everything was perfect. At sunset, there was a bonfire around which children holding long burning sticks shrieked and danced, and they watched them leaping through the dark orange under the stars.

Later, the two of them sat there together and she said, I'm a funny one, Noah, and Noah said, How's that? and she said, That's what they say, then smiled at him and reached out and wiggled her fingers in front of his face then put her hand in the fire.

After what seemed like quite some time, though probably was not—Noah told himself later that night as he drove home that it couldn't have been—she pulled it out and said, touch it, and Noah did, and she laughed and said, Funny like that, and Noah leaned over and put his lips on her cheek, then said, Let's go put some cold water on that hand, and she said, All right, Noah Summers, and together they watched the cold water pour over the gently curled fingers of her upturned hand.

In the autumn he helped her family (though not her parents, they, she had told him, were one hundred percent deceased), though he cannot this moment remember a single one of them, cut and press sugarcane. A fog, said the Minister, on Sunday, as they sat together, quietly together, will pass across each face. He remembers hers.

She is fine, said Ruby.

Yes, said Virgil.

Noah asked them to repeat this, to promise this, and, as he has often since remembered, they did.

After much consultation between Virgil and Ruby and the Spears, it was decided that given the circumstances, which included that the two parties had become inseparable, but also that the bride had done a spell at Logansport and the groom had clear eccentricities of his own, a union of sorts was in order, but that involving the church and the county should wait. Virgil would take full responsibility for the situation and after a trial run they would see about the other formalities.

I don't care what you call it, we'll be married, said Noah.

That's what we'll say, Virgil said.

Man and wife, said Noah. I'll love her forever.

I know you will, Ruby said.

After the ceremony, which was presided over by Virgil and attended by Ruby and Opal's stepfather, Ralph Spears, whose only counsel to Opal, after Virgil's rather lengthy invocations of Plato and Seneca and Michel de Montaigne, was that she damn well better behave, they set off on their honeymoon to a cave in Kentucky that Virgil and Ruby had taken Noah to several years before. Virgil and Ruby, who accompanied them, just to make sure everything went smoothly, took a room down the hall and told them to go out and enjoy both themselves and the sights.

They walked through the town. They sat at a counter and ate ham sandwiches with too much mustard on them. They took a tour of the big cave, walking shoulder to shoulder, holding hands.

She said it was just like the stalactites and stalagmites that grew together in beautiful pink columns.

What is?

Us walking together, like this, holding hands.

The tour took them deep into the cave and past a passage that was roped off.

Come on, said Opal.

They waited until the others had rounded a bend then stepped under the rope and went down the narrow passage and under another rope and saw the prow of a boat.

Opal wanted to get into the boat and Noah wanted to go wherever Opal wanted so they started to move forward but a man came up behind them and asked them if they wouldn't care to rejoin the tour.

I want to get in that boat, Opal said.

Cave boat's closed today, Ma'am, the man said.

Opal smiled. My name is Opal, this here is my new husband Noah, she said. It's our honeymoon. I would like to get on that boat and take a ride down the dark river under the earth.

The man looked at them. He smiled. He had a nephew who had just gotten married. He said, Follow me. And as the boat slid along the dark, smooth water, the man tipped his hat back and began to sing.

Then for a time they lived together.

And in the evening they rode through the fields in the truck. There were daylilies in the ditches and clouds of butterflies and blue chicory and when they drove by people waved and they waved back and once they rode out to the lake where Noah had fallen through the ice and they swam and Opal said let's sink and they sank and on the dark sandy bottom they held hands.

During the day Opal would help Ruby around the house or out in the yard or garden and Ruby said she was smart "my good Lord she is something smart" and some evenings the four of them would sit down to supper and Virgil would talk and Opal would listen and Virgil would ask her questions and she would answer and Noah would help clear the table and Ruby would wink at him and Noah would wink back and they would have dessert then help with the dishes then walk the hundred yards back to their house.

At night they lay together in the big bed by the window there were flowers in the room they had set tulips out in the bed by the front porch Noah said I don't know and Opal said You will know I promise and Noah said I'm not sure and she said I promise and the bed spun Noah told her it was spinning and she said yes and Noah said nothing saw nothing just her just their house just the gently spinning bed.

One evening Virgil came late and sat with them on their porch a breeze was blowing and Noah said Welcome to our porch and Virgil said Thank you and poured them each a finger of blackjack Strictly medicinal you understand and Opal said We understand she wore a blue gingham dress Ruby had bought her for a wedding present the breeze blew it around her ankles and off in the distance there were thunderclouds they watched the lightning and Virgil said Maybe there'll be a storm and then there was and as they watched it she said it looked like diamonds exploding and that it was so pretty and that she was so glad they were all alive and that they weren't all dead.

One morning, one month and ten days after the wedding, June 22, 1937, Opal stood up from the kitchen table, went into the bedroom, lay down on the bed, went still for a moment, then started screaming. For one hour, she did not stop screaming.

And that evening when Noah came home, the house, their house, was burning.

Noah found her sitting in the kitchen, one hand on the table the other in her lap. Two of the walls had caught and long fingers of hot smoke were coming in under the pantry door, but she looked at Noah and, just like she did every evening, smiled and welcomed him.

I'm sorry, but I set the curtains on fire, Noah, what would you like for supper, your folks will be along any time now and I haven't gotten anything started, she said.

We're leaving honey, we're leaving right now, Noah said.

We don't have to do that, there's no real reason to leave just this second, Noah, Opal said.

Now, said Noah.

Opal reached out and grabbed the edges of the table and Noah said Are you coming or not and Opal said that no she wasn't coming and the pantry door was now on fire right in the center of it was a black and orange ring Noah could hear Virgil and Ruby calling outside come on now he said Opal who was now screaming again in the end he had to pry her fingers off the edges of the table then half drag half carry her screaming out onto the lawn.

Dear Noah,

she said. The last time he saw her. She was an old woman then. There were big windows and a sweet scent to the air and plush green carpets covering the floors.

Like the fields but not like the fields do you remember them Noah?
    yes
and the black dirt?
    yes
the black dirt and being barefoot and not hearing your footsteps only feeling them?
    yes
did it rain Noah?
did it pour Dear Noah?
    yes
    yes
    yes

THERE IS A CANE PRESS standing somewhere out in the yard. Noah can't think where. He vaguely remembers having found it once, hidden behind a scrub mulberry that grew up between two scorched foundation stones where the little house used to stand, then becomes aware that he has fallen back into the half sleep, and that this time the people stand inside the wall, and it is they, not the walls, who are translucent. Noah watches them shimmer then fade slowly, until their translucency is absolute.

Dear Noah,

It has rained all day. I had hoped I would see hummingbirds at the new feeder but none came. Least ways not while I was watching. Maybe they don't like the wet. What do you think? They're so tiny—like pretty thoughts. I am sending you someone. His name is Max, Noah. He came while I was watching for the hummingbirds and I said hello I don't know you and he said no you don't and I said well. He said who he was and I said he had better go and see you. He said he would like that and I sat there and thought about it. He was a nice fellow, Noah. He was so nice and brought me lilies and after a while put his hand on mine. Gentle like. I looked at his fingers and thought about it and said I was sorry and he said it was all right but I just went ahead and looked at his fingers and said I was sorry until I had said it a hundred times.

Love, Opal

IT IS NOW 4:30 IN THE MORNING and Noah is drinking from a small stone jug that he keeps on the floor beside the chair. Inside the jug is a wine Noah makes in the autumn from a grape vine that came up volunteer along the edge of the garden. The wine is dark and strong and in the early morning before he works Noah likes to sit by the stove and take small sips of it. Some days in the winter when there are no jobs around the farm, or even when there are, Noah spends the whole day sitting by the stove taking small sips from the jug. But today, at first light, he needs to pick up the saw and the ladder and set out across the field. There are seven branches that need cutting. Noah has counted them. They are covered with ice and have been bent too close to an electric power line that runs over to Zorrie Underwood's. If one of the jagged ice-laden branches snaps, the line could be severed. Noah has seen a severed power line. It looked like a huge welding torch gone awry, or like something out of one of the books Virgil used to read to him.

And when they come it will be for cleansing.

Who is they?

I don't know, let me keep reading.

The snapped power line spit white fire for three hours before the county turned it off. This happened after Virgil had stopped talking and stopped reading aloud and used to take a stool and a weed-sickle and walk back into the fields. Noah found him standing just beyond the reach of the snaking line.

You will pass through six blue arches, Virgil read, years before, then slip through six blue walls.

How do they know that?

They don't—of course, they don't. But it could be.

There's lots of things that could be.

Plenty that couldn't, for that matter.

Like Heaven?

I didn't say that.

I don't think there's any Heaven.

Don't tell your mother that.

Do you?

Virgil raised his eyebrow.

I think there's something. But it's not Heaven.

What is it?

Noah shrugged. I don't know. I reckon by and by we'll see.

It was Max who told Noah about the power line and the tree. On clear afternoons Max goes out walking in the fields. Noah has seen his tracks in the snow and sometimes he follows them. Most often they lead out into the middle of a field and stop. There Noah can see where Max stood until the snow froze under his boots or where he sat or lay in the snow, and once Noah, too, for the first time in years, stretched himself out on the soft cold earth and looked up into the cloudless sky. Another time he followed Max's winding tracks across the snowy bean stubble and the rolling expanse of the big field, through the South Woods, and out onto the surface of the water that covers the gravel pit, the discovery and subsequent sale of which finally permitted Noah to move Opal out of the hospital and into a rest home. The tracks led into the middle of the pit, and there Noah could see where Max had knelt and cleared away the snow. The wind had blown a light layer of granular crystals back over the spot so Noah, too, took his hand and brushed it clean. He leaned forward, smiled. Max had scraped "I'll bring supper over" into the dark gray surface of the ice.

Max brought over pork chops, mashed potatoes, frozen peas, and two fat slices of blueberry pie, and when they were finished eating, he made a pot of coffee, set the cups on the table, leaned back in his chair, and said, You know she never held it against you. She never held it against Virgil either. According to what she told me—and forget what her records said—she would've just kept on with it. Like as not it would've been worse the next time. Getting her into where they could help her was the best thing anyone could have done.

That's not the first time I heard that, Noah said. No, said Max. I expect not.

More than one's told me about that being best. That it was best my wife was put away. That it was best no one saw fit to tell me there was more to it than just my wife.

Max looked at Noah. He took a sip of his coffee.

I suppose they have, he said.

They have, said Noah.

Max nodded.

What about you? Noah said. You reckon their incarcerating her was the best thing for you?

Max took another sip of his coffee, poured himself some more, looked around the room, then leaned back on his chair again.

Well, he said. Then he shrugged. Then he said, I suppose I made out all right. I don't know. They let me keep my name. First name anyway. I got treated pretty fair, didn't get moved around too much. I always knew about Opal. I expect that given the circumstances at the time, what with her gone and you having your own difficulties, it was probably the best thing for me too.

Probably, said Noah. I got up to plenty of my own foolishness and wasn't entirely fit for company. I reckon that hasn't changed.

Noah smiled, then reached for his coffee, then set the cup back down without drinking and put his forehead against his hand. After a moment he looked up again.

Funny thing is I still loved him afterward.

Virgil?

I tried. I even thought once or twice about killing him. That's how crazy I got. But it wouldn't stick.

No, I don't suppose it would.

I held out pretty hard against him though. Harder than I sometimes wished I had.

It wasn't . . .

Wasn't his fault. Wasn't her step-folks' fault either. I know that. I reckon part of me knows that. She wrote me not long after and said as much. Said there wasn't nobody but her, if you had to have someone, to blame.

Max leaned forward.

I was going to say it wasn't your fault.

Well, said Noah, and chuckled, briefly. She said that too. Then after that she said something about a flying shovel and a giant turtle with a golden shell, or some such. I suppose in the end it all works out about the same.

HERE IS ANOTHER VERSION. Just as the conception of the Ark was pinioned on sets of two, so, like the image in a slightly warped mirror, there was another Noah, one who had also built a fine enough ship at God's bidding, only to his ark no animals came. Nor did wife or child come and when he searched the hills and dales he found that all those he had known and loved in his life had vanished. So that when the rains began to fall in earnest and the deluge commenced this Noah found himself lifted up and carried across the waters alone. Those forty days and forty nights passed for this Noah as they did for the other only, passed in solitude, they seemed a hundredfold as long. When at last the rains stopped, and the Sun appeared, he found himself adrift for many days in a great, deep ocean and was quickly plunged again into numbness and despair. And while he sat thus aimlessly on the deck one morning it seemed to him he saw a bird approach: a crow with an olive sprig in its beak. Hungry and too deluded to realize what to the other would seem explicit, this Noah coaxed the exhausted bird toward him, then killed, half-plucked, and ate it. After he had eaten it he retired to his cabin and fell immediately into strange and bottomless dreams, and so did not see, off toward the horizon, another ark, much like his, that had just raised full sail, nor did he hear the cry of wonder that arose from its decks.

Outside, the service light has switched itself off, and the light that now filters in through the small frozen window is sickly and gray. Noah has taken up the mask and, after staring into its eyeless face for a time, has flipped it over and slipped it on. Wearing the mask, he pictures himself, an old man with a strange, bedeviled face, moving across the field carrying the saw, rope, and ladder, and climbing into the tree.

The day before he fell over in the kitchen, Virgil lay in bed with his eyes softly burning and, speaking up out of his deep silence, said to Noah, Forget what I ever told you, directions will be given, and afterwards, after the funeral, Ruby, leaning on Noah's arm as they stood in the yard and looked out across the empty fields, said, Stay on this farm. Noah remembers a television program in which an old man returning to his home of many years from a series of long journeys is visited by winged versions of all the people he has loved and lost during his life. When the old man asks one of them why they visit him here instead of elsewhere, the blue-winged woman tells him they could never have found him otherwise.

Why did you want to find me? the old man asks.

We have things to tell you, dear, the woman says.

A cat brushes up against Noah's leg as he stands by the window, but this time he ignores it and, looking out into the endless acres of white, lets his mind move back to the tree. The big saw is tinted blue with cold, and Noah's bulky three- and four-fingered gloves make holding it difficult. He sees himself stopping to rest halfway through the first branch, sees his quick breath turning to steam, and sees the power line humming below. He adjusts the rope, removes the mask, takes a deep breath of cold, clean air, then lets himself fall, crashing, up or down through the tree.

NOW I WANT YOU TO LISTEN TO ME.

Noah nodded. They were sitting on the stump watching the tractor steam.

You remember what I told you a palimpsest was?

You never told me.

Yes I did, but never mind. It's something shot through with something else. Does that ring any bell?

Noah looked at him.

You never told me.

All right, never mind. I once read about a town where they didn't have doctors, they had a law. The law was that anyone sick was laid out in the center of town and everyone passing by had to stop and say whether or not they had ever suffered similarly and if they had what they had done and what advice they in turn had received. Now, I don't know whether a chicken or an egg got hatched out of that situation, but I do know that when they were done lying there they were either on their way to being better or they weren't. Which makes it about fifty percent clear and fifty percent not. And which accords with the fact that I have yet to acquaint myself with any history or parable that does not either leave it all sitting where it is which is in darkness or semidarkness or try to wrap it all up neat. This is not neat. And I do not know how to make it so.

Virgil took a deep breath.

I did not want to be in that position, I did not ask to be in that position, but I was, and if, as I am told it has sometimes been granted, I had it to do over again, I do not know that I would do it differently, that fire she set and whatever else was burning in her was just too hot. That is not meant to be taken as an endorsement of that fool Galton's theories of inferiority and such like. And you should not allow yourself to continue with the impression that I was too hateful to be bothered by the sorry, sorry knowledge we have of what can and does take place in such institutions in the name of salubriousness. But there was and is no means to place her in better circumstances and into circumstances of some stripe she did have to be placed. You know as well as I do that she was as lucid as a gas flame set to high when she was lucid and that she herself endorsed, and more than once, the course that we took. She wrote you that and she wrote me the same. Any argument there?

Noah said nothing.

But I am sorry. For all of it. Not least that I relinquished the custody to her people and they thought it best to shut you out. Over and over I am sorry. Just as sorry as I was when I used to run off and carry on. Your mother came pretty close to hating me over that, told me so, slapped my face, threw my hat on the burning pile.

On the burning pile? said Noah.

Virgil nodded.

You saying you running around and playing cards with folks and women sets the same as what got done to Opal?

Virgil shook his head.

My point's not there and I expect you know that. Shall I continue or do you want to discuss it?

Go on, said Noah.

Anyway, I couldn't blame her, just like I can't blame you for what your thinking about me is.

Are you asking? said Noah.

Are you interested in answering? said Virgil.

No.

Then, no. Now, your mother might lay a different slant on this after I'm gone, and I may change my mind on it in about an hour anyway, but right now, right this second, I will tell you again, like I been saying your whole life and now much of my own, that if something approximating understanding is what you are after, and I think that is what you are after, then you best not hold your breath, because if any helpful apparition is going to come down out of those clouds or out of that stump or out of that cup of dried bittersweet your mother keeps on the counter and hand you an answer key, it will likely come too heavily encrypted to make heads or tails out of, like a breviary of sacred phrases in one of the Hittite dialects, or a map of the stars in Chinese.

RUBY DID NOT LAY MUCH of a slant on it at all, although when for a brief period of time between Virgil's and Ruby's deaths people began arriving, Ruby served them hot coffee or lemonade as the season warranted before retiring to her Bible and television, which she kept tuned, as frequently as possible, to the news (when it was time for the weather) or to game shows.

Noah would sit with them on the back porch or in the kitchen or on the stone benches in front of the house. The first to come was a retired pumpkin farmer from Carroll County who had been three months at Logansport and wanted to know just how many more hours he had until he would be "sitting upstairs with the good Lord," and when Noah said he didn't know, which was true, they just sat there together and watched the road, and the pumpkin farmer told Noah about his truck, which he had bought from his cousin's wife's uncle for $40 and was now worth $4,000. Next was a Frankfort Cigar Company man whose sister's friend had sent him to inquire after a boy she had lost "out on the ice" (in this case, although he did not say it, Noah had seen something: a small, preternaturally circular, frozen face), and after that it was a woman in wedding shoes with electrical tape on her teeth.

I knew that gal, said Ruby after the woman had left. Laetitia. Used to have a pretty voice. Pretty as pearls. That's what we'd say. She used to sing up at Cousin Ella's church. What did you tell her?

Noah shrugged. Ruby nodded.

Opal's sending them. She's telling them about you. I know that's why you won't stop it, and they'll keep coming, and I'll keep serving them lemonade. I ought to charge.

She did not charge and, after a while, when Opal, as they sometimes told him she would ("the last time I saw her she was sitting by the door with a suitcase" or "every time I talked to her she kept talking about the farm," or "she would say things like 'it is pretty there when the wind blows,' and 'when you walk in the summer the high grasses brush against your hands'"), did not come home, Noah stopped answering the door.

Max, who came much later than the others (though not, or only indirectly, from the state hospital), and has stayed in the area much longer, solved that problem by not knocking.

I did not want to impose upon you, he said, the daily necessity of having to decide whether or not to let your son come in.

AFTER OPAL HAD BEEN TAKEN TO LOGANSPORT—while Noah was delivering a truckload of straw to Kempton—Noah spent a day then a night then half a morning in the South Woods, before setting out to see the Spears.

We been involved, they said, showing him a small stack of letters from Virgil, the latest of which had advised them, they informed Noah, that in view of the fire, and the incidents mentioned in his previous correspondence, that he had been obliged to involve the authorities in the situation. Certain papers had had to be signed by himself and by the family and they had signed them.

What other incidents? Noah said.

You want me to read you these letters?

I'm her damn family, said Noah. Apparently all she's got that's worth anything.

It ain't the first time she's had to rest up for a while, and you know it, Noah. Least this way she'll be somewhere they can take care of her.

Take care of her? said Noah. You know what they'll do to her up there, don't you? They'll do all kinds of damn things to her.

Now, Noah, they said. You come on in and we'll get you some supper, then we'll give your daddy a call.

But Noah was already walking.

He made Howard County before 10:00 p.m., lay down in a ditch outside Oakford, shivered for a while, thought too much, then slept. By 4:00 a.m. he was walking again and by 6:00 a.m. he was on the outskirts of Kokomo breakfasting on what was presented to him as "just some played-out biscuits and cold coffee" with a fellow named Steve Shanks, who said he was on his way up to South Bend to see if he could get hired back on at Studebaker and wouldn't mind sharing some of the stretch. They knocked their way through the biscuits, and Shanks talked and after they had walked a while, Shanks talking up a job he'd once had outside Union City and a sweet little number he'd "some ways known," Noah said he wasn't necessarily feeling social and that he'd best keep on alone.

That's all right, said Shanks. I'm feeling social enough for the both of us.

Noah shrugged, and they walked, and after a time Shanks had Noah talking.

I think I might of killed my daddy if he'd done that behind my back.

I thought of that, said Noah.

I bet you did, said Shanks.

But she did just about burn us down.

True, but that don't change the principle.

Noah nodded.

You think you can get her back out?

That's what I'm fixing to investigate.

They slept in the ruins of a corncrib within earshot of the frogs crowding Wildcat Creek and woke to the scolding of a jay that had set up its shop in a hickory that was growing its way over the mess of coon-chewed cobs and rotten boards. Noah blinked and looked over at Shanks who lay snoring in a puddle of sun and for three or four happy minutes had no idea who or where he was. This lasted until he bent over the smoothly running surface of the creek and saw the dark reflection of his face. When the subject of breakfast came up, Noah said he had money and Shanks said, Why didn't you holler? and they cut across a weed-killed field of beans, down a stretch of dirt and gravel, onto a paved road, into Burlington, and up to the door of a breakfast counter Shanks knew.

Shanks said, after you, Mr. President, and they sat down to eggs and biscuits with sausage gravy, which was brought to them by a waitress who Shanks called darling and told Noah he admired.

I like bigger gals, Shanks said.

Noah put a piece of egg into his mouth, followed it up with some biscuit, and chewed.

Shanks thought that since they were paying customers they ought to linger, but Noah said he had to get walking.

About that, said Shanks. If you got to get up there and you got money, why ain't you accommodating yourself?

We got a truck at home, I could've took that, said Noah.

Shanks whistled. You got a truck and you got money and you're sleeping in corncribs and wearing your shoes out.

I don't know what I'm going to do yet.

Do? said Shanks. That's your wife up there. You go on up and sign papers and she comes home then you kill your daddy and your momma too, I reckon.

It's complicated, said Noah.

Complicated! Bring us some more coffee, darling. I got a man here says money and a truck is complicated.

The waitress came, poured, and went back behind the counter. Shanks took a drink, let out a little moan of satisfaction, then leaned back in his seat and said, You ain't in trouble in the law direction, are you?

Noah said he'd rather not talk about it.

Shanks said he understood but wouldn't mind clarifying, if it was all the same, having had his run-ins, that Noah wasn't about to get himself pickled up.

I haven't done anything, not yet, said Noah.

Then that's fine, said Shanks.

They drank a while, and Shanks made his attempt with the waitress, apologized to her, tried to turn her acceptance of the apology to his advantage, just about got himself slapped, placed another order, was ignored, sang a little song about daylilies, then suggested they go.

I got certain particulars to take account of, said Noah.

Particulars?

Particulars so that any paper has to be signed by my daddy and her family for it to be legal.

What kind of particulars, exactly?

Health particulars. To do with my comportment.

Shanks took a deep breath and looked at Noah, interested.

You crazy, son? You got your bolts loose?

That's why it don't make sense that they took her and not me. They should've at least took us both.

You get violent, son? said Shanks. You tear things up and howl at the Moon?

I see things.

See things how?

And have fits.

You shucking me?

I fall over and forget where I am. Virgil says it's a special state. Says I got something extra. I say it's just me, pure and crazy. Crazy since the day I was born.

Virgil's the one you aim to kill?

I ain't going to kill him, let's leave off that.

Shanks said that was wisest, that killing never amounted to anything but trouble.

You ever kill anyone? asked Noah.

Not yet, said Shanks.

Noah nodded. They walked. Noah thought about Virgil. Shanks whistled. He held forth for a time on the subject of the automobile industry in Indiana, then asked Noah what kind of things he saw.

All kinds. Most don't matter. Never happened, never will. They're just figments.

By this time they were on the Michigan Road and getting toward Wheeling, and Shanks had his thumb out as often as there were vehicles, but none stopped.

Shanks said he didn't like the sound of figments, not one bit, but wondered if Noah had seen anything to do with him.

You like hummingbirds, said Noah.

Lord almighty, that's a fact. My momma was partial to them. Set out sugar water in a red dish. I was bunking outside Plymouth and had a hummingbird land on my nose. That all?

That's all and that ain't much seeing as how you called that gal back there your "little hummingbird" when you were according her your gallantries.

Shanks said, Well . . . then laughed and did a little dance he called "gallantries," and they went on, and Noah didn't tell him what he had seen and hoped he would not see it again and that it would never come to pass.

That night, they set up in an oak grove just north of Clymers, and while they tossed brush onto their little fire and smacked away at mosquitoes not put off by the heat and smoke, Noah told Shanks little bits and pieces about Opal, about how bright she was, which people referred to as "different," and also about the dogwood tree she had pulled all the blossoms off, and of course the fire, which had scared him pretty good, and still scared him a little, when, he told Shanks, he saw her sitting there at the table with the smoking door behind her.

I never been involved in a fire, said Shanks. What's it like?

What's it like? said Noah.

Shanks in turn told Noah about his own great love. This "real big gal" had to his everlasting regret married the owner of a dry goods store, a mean old coot who had taken exception to Shanks for "once or twice" at most "mooning around" the shop, where Lucilla spent her weekday afternoons spooning jam out of jars and into her mouth and attending to the cash register. Despite the interference of the husband, Shanks had managed to continue to press his suit, with so much success that one afternoon while the husband was down in the cellar checking stock, Lucilla told him to meet her that very evening down at the park. That Lucilla "in all her perfume and glory" had not appeared and that four persuasive gentlemen of her husband's acquaintance had, in no way negatively colored Shanks's memory of his gal.

How long did you run around with her before she got married?

Shanks sighed and chewed absently at a hangnail.

Well, speaking factually, it was all more or less from a distance and just talking. I used to see her consorting with various of her amicales at the sundae parlor. I only talked to her but once or twice. There wasn't really much running around to it at all.

They talked on, or Shanks did. He said Indiana was the greatest state in the country, and Noah, admitting it didn't seem all that great to him just now, asked him why he thought so.

Why is Indiana the greatest state in the country? That's what I'm asking.

Shanks shrugged.

I don't know. It's home. It's where we're stuck. Anyway, sounds good, don't it?

Indiana, said Noah.

Indiana, said Shanks.

The fire died and rose. They caught sight of what might have been a bat flicking through the trees. Shanks said that made him think of something and started singing a tune about a lady in Indiana with a bat in her hair but broke off.

It's all right, said Noah.

Well . . . said Shanks.

Keep on singing, said Noah.

Shanks reached out his hand and placed it lightly on Noah's shoulder then retracted it and went back to singing and sang until he had fallen into a doze and Noah watched the fire then could no longer stand it and went off and walked a while through the dark.

Late the next morning they arrived in Logansport, which was home, Shanks informed Noah, to more than one notable gas-buggy works, including Victor Bendix's famous plant.

I might just wander over to one or another of them after a spell and see what's what, said Shanks.

Sounds fine, said Noah.

I mean when we got you square, said Shanks.

I appreciate that, said Noah.

You hungry?

I didn't think I would be but I am.

After they had lunched on creamed corn and tenderloin sandwiches, Shanks asked Noah if he had it figured yet, and Noah said he reckoned he'd just try and see what trying accomplished. Shanks asked him if he wanted company while he tried, but Noah said it was best now he went alone.

You might want to smooth down your hair and fetch you up some soap before you head over, said Shanks. Doctors and such are particular.

There's that word again, said Noah.

There it is, said Shanks.

Noah thanked him then, over Shanks's lukewarm pro-
tests, reached into his pocket and brought out half of what he
had left.

That's more than enough, said Shanks.

I don't need it, Noah said. Anyway, I'm not necessarily
supposed to have this money. And if I don't have it when I'm
asked for it, which I will be, I won't be able to return it, and
that won't hurt anything, the way I'm figuring.

Amen, said Shanks.

I reckon amen don't have anything to do with it, said Noah.

No, I reckon it don't.

They shook hands and Shanks did another little dance
then bowed and wished Noah good luck.

Noah took a room in a little hotel that boasted fine dining and
clean facilities and after he had taken the direct opposite of
Shanks's advice and mussed himself up even more, he made
his way up to the hospital, where every day, until the guards
received instructions not to allow him to enter, he attempted,
once smacking his fist down in the middle of a pile of papers
a doctor refused to take his attention away from, to persuade
the doctors to let him exchange places with Opal.

I'm her God damn husband, Noah said.

We are more than aware of the several dimensions of the
situation, Mr. Summers.

You'll at least let me see her again. I want to see her.

That would be inadvisable at the current stage, Mr.
Summers.

I don't care how advisable it is.

Inadvisable, Mr. Summers, means impossible, at the current stage. Miss Spears's situation is very, very serious, as you
have seen for yourself, and as I have underscored.

You've got her plied with drugs and such.

We offer the finest recuperative facilities in the state and she will, you have my assurance, be well cared for. For as long, Mr. Summers, as that is deemed necessary. Your father, who holds the guardianship with her family . . .

I don't care about guardianship. She's married. She's married to me. It was a real marriage. Just as good as real. I want to see her again right this second.

Now, Mr. Summers, *please* . . .

That night, after the guards had escorted him off the property, he sat with his cheek pressed against the window of the small hotel room looking out at the street and the illuminated buildings beyond. Below him, a young, well-dressed woman was standing in the street waving to a car that was pulling away. The woman stood and waved sadly, but then, when the car was gone, she turned, took two slow steps toward the curb, and, instead of a taking a third slow step, she looked over her shoulder, straightened, laughed, and leapt onto the sidewalk with an energy so unexpected, so incomprehensible to Noah, like so much of what had happened, that it slapped him away from the window and into the far corner of the dark hotel room. There, he sat holding himself very, very still, much as he would sit (prevented by official order, at the request of Opal's family, from seeing his wife, who, he would learn only many years later, when a tall man named Max came and knocked on his side door, had been carrying their child) in the months to come at home in the dark barn, wracked with the sensation that the floor was falling, any floor, all floors, and he with it. When the next day, Virgil, who had received a phone call from the hospital, came to collect him, Noah tried screaming, but could not sustain it—he went quiet when his father took him by the shoulders, leaned close to him, and whispered, hush. Much later, when, suddenly awake in the middle of the night, Noah tried screaming again, he found that he could, in fact, sustain it, but by that time, and he soon fell silent, anyone who might have heard him had gone.

Dear Noah,

Come soon. It is all so beautiful. Indiana is beautiful. Indiana where the lilacs are flowering. Indiana where the furrows are sprouting fireflies and corn. Last night I had a dream in which the little courtyard here was filled with cakes of soap. Then it rained and the soap bubbled up over us and we were clean and afterwards Moses wrote about it, a long, long story over the course of which our hips grew wider and our skulls grew thinner, until someone sent someone else down to make dirt paintings out of us, after which we took off our old faces, hid them away, then rose and went running forever across great fields that were gold.

Love, Opal

AT SEVEN O'CLOCK, NOAH WAKES from a brief dreamless sleep and, though he does not know why, smiles. Smiling, he stands, buttons his coat, takes off the mask, crosses the room, puts the mask in the dresser on the piece of butcher paper, touches the forehead of the face beside it, and shuts the drawer. Then, holding his back very straight, he pulls down the saw, returns to the chair in front of the fire, and sits. This time he does not sleep. With the saw in his hands and the mask now sitting beside Opal's in the dresser, he again has the feeling that he is mounted on something very old, something that he cannot see and will not see that is breaking into a gallop. Noah shuts his eyes, takes a deep breath, and, as he does so, finds he is reminded of the time that he and Opal rode in the boat over the dark water with the man singing songs behind them. As they rounded a long bend, the man began to sing a song they both knew, about moonlight and a river, and, after looking at each other and leaning closer, they joined him. Noah joins them.

ONCE, AS A BOY, Noah went alone into a purple tent at the county fair to have his palm read. The palm reader, who was an older girl from another school district, looked carefully at his face and touched the inside of his hand. Then, in an unnaturally deep voice, she told him he would be a great football player someday. Strangely, though he never became a football player, when several years later he lost the fingers, the first to an adze, the others to a combine, and, nothing having changed, it seemed to him everything in his life had gone awry, Noah thought immediately of the palm reader. After the second incident, he tried to find her. Her mother, however, told him that she had left the county straight after high school, and—not at all surprisingly, thought Noah—had given no news of herself since.

ACKNOWLEDGMENTS

Indiana, Indiana is a work of fiction. The people and circumstances it describes were imagined.

Many books informed and inspired this one. Among these were *Angel in the Forest* by Marguerite Young; *Coming Through Slaughter* by Michael Ondaatje; *Mad in America* by Robert Whitaker; *The Play-Party in Indiana: A Collection of Folk-Songs and Games* by Leah Jackson Wolford; *Raintree County* by Ross Lockridge Jr.; *The Persian Wars* by Herodotus; *With Custer on the Little Bighorn* by William O. Taylor; *Pedro Páramo* by Juan Rulfo; *The Rings of Saturn* by W. G. Sebald; and *Memoirs of Hadrian* by Marguerite Yourcenar.

Virgil's remarks about vowels and birds are adapted from "Notes prises pour un oiseau," which appears in *La Rage de l'expression* by Francis Ponge. Virgil's thoughts on time were inspired by Clark Coolidge's poem "Done," which can be found in *Sound as Thought: Poems 1982–1984.*

I am particularly indebted to the Cass County Historical Society in Logansport, Indiana, for steering me to the excellent Longcliff Museum (and its wonderful staff) attached to the Logansport State Hospital. A number of particularly fruitful hours were spent at the Frankfort Public Library, in Frankfort, Indiana.

Bits of family lore and history informed aspects of certain characters and events. Many thanks especially to my great-grandfather Virgil Burnau, whose erudition, legendary loquacity, and several other particulars (though in no way his beliefs, actions, or state of mind) helped shape my character of the same first name.

This book could not have been written had I not spent five years living on a farm in rural Indiana with my beloved grandmother Helen Burnau Hunt, who taught me many things, including to look for cardinals in the dead of winter, flying over the snow, shining red against the dark trunks.

Coffee House Press began as a small letterpress operation in 1972 and has grown into an internationally renowned non-profit publisher of literary fiction, essay, poetry, and other work that doesn't fit neatly into genre categories.

Coffee House is both a publisher and an arts organization. Through our *Books in Action* program and publications, we've become interdisciplinary collaborators and incubators for new work and audience experiences. Our vision for the future is one where a publisher is a catalyst and connector.

LITERATURE
is not the same thing as
PUBLISHING

FUNDER ACKNOWLEDGMENTS

Coffee House Press is an internationally renowned independent book publisher and arts nonprofit based in Minneapolis, MN; through its literary publications and *Books in Action* program, Coffee House acts as a catalyst and connector—between authors and readers, ideas and resources, creativity and community, inspiration and action.

Coffee House Press books are made possible through the generous support of grants and donations from corporations, state and federal grant programs, family foundations, and the many individuals who believe in the transformational power of literature. This activity is made possible by the voters of Minnesota through a Minnesota State Arts Board Operating Support grant, thanks to the legislative appropriation from the Arts and Cultural Heritage Fund. Coffee House also receives major operating support from the Amazon Literary Partnership, Jerome Foundation, Literary Arts Emergency Fund, McKnight Foundation, and the National Endowment for the Arts (NEA). To find out more about how NEA grants impact individuals and communities, visit www.arts.gov.

Coffee House Press receives additional support from Bookmobile; Dorsey & Whitney LLP; Elmer L. & Eleanor J. Andersen Foundation; the Matching Grant Program Fund of the Minneapolis Foundation; Mr. Pancks' Fund in memory of Graham Kimpton; the Schwab Charitable Fund; and the U.S. Bank Foundation.

THE PUBLISHER'S CIRCLE OF
COFFEE HOUSE PRESS

Publisher's Circle members make significant contributions to Coffee House Press's annual giving campaign. Understanding that a strong financial base is necessary for the press to meet the challenges and opportunities that arise each year, this group plays a crucial part in the success of Coffee House's mission.

Recent Publisher's Circle members include many anonymous donors, Patricia A. Beithon, Anitra Budd, Andrew Brantingham, Kelli & Dave Cloutier, Mary Ebert & Paul Stembler, Kamilah Foreman, Jocelyn Hale & Glenn Miller Charitable Fund of the Minneapolis Foundation, the Rehael Fund-Roger Hale/Nor Hall of the Minneapolis Foundation, Randy Hartten & Ron Lotz, Dylan Hicks & Nina Hale, William Hardacker, Kenneth & Susan Kahn, the Kenneth Koch Literary Estate, Cinda Kornblum, Jennifer Kwon Dobbs & Stefan Liess, the Lenfestey Family Foundation, Sarah Lutman & Rob Rudolph, the Carol & Aaron Mack Charitable Fund of the Minneapolis Foundation, Gillian McCain, Mary & Malcolm McDermid, Daniel N. Smith III & Maureen Millea Smith, Enrique & Jennifer Olivarez, Robin Preble, Nan G. Swid, Grant Wood, and Margaret Wurtele.

For more information about the Publisher's Circle and other ways to support Coffee House Press books, authors, and activities, please visit www.coffeehousepress.org/pages/donate or contact us at info@coffeehousepress.org.